Masters of Paradise

POPPY FLYNN

Poppy Flynn

Copyright

Foreword

Meet the Masters of Paradise.

Ten men and women who invest in the creation of a very special holiday resort named Eden on the tropical island of Elysium.

This uninhabited, private island is set to become a kink lovers paradise with its very own BDSM club which goes by the name of *Iniquity*.

Within these pages you'll get a glimpse into the back story of each character. You'll get see what drives them and find out how they all came to be part of this brand new venture.

Look out for their stories and read about all of them as supporting characters in each others books.

Temptation Book 1 in the *Masters of Paradise* series is available now.

In the beginning

Luca Moreno, his lovers Ryan, and Zoe Moore, and seven of their friends looked out over the island the ten of them had just purchased.

Relatively speaking, it was surprising how inexpensive it was to buy a private island in the Bahamas. This one hadn't been the cheapest, but in the grand scheme of things, the nine-million-dollar price tag was a drop in the ocean. Just like the island itself.

Or a jewel, as he preferred to think of it.

It didn't look like much right now. Despite the golden beaches and the lush stretch of green which meandered down the hillside either side of a natural stream, there was enough rock and scrub in between to make much of it look fairly inhospitable.

There were just flashes of brilliance, but you had to have a vision for the rest of it.

Or blind faith.

It wasn't paradise right now, but it would be.

Fortunately, he had the necessary vision as well as the expertise, along with his cousin, Daniella, who was also onboard, after fifteen years working for his father's resort chain. And the rest of them had enough faith in their experience to part with substantial amounts of money.

Buying Elysium Island was just the first step. Right now, it was uninhabited and didn't even have an infrastructure. They were going to have to establish things like electricity and a proper water supply before they could even start building.

Two hotels, one on each side of the three by five-mile island, both complete with bars, restaurants, and a pool. Extensive employee accommodation since the staff was going to have to live onsite. A golf course, a spa, and an outdoor, open air entertainment venue. A harbour and water sports complex, with a cafe. Probably a couple of small shops for staff and visitors alike to pick up little bits and pieces they'd forgotten, or emergency supplies and another one selling tourist memorabilia. A medical centre and a helipad would be essential since they were eighty miles from the mainland. And in the bowels of each hotel, a casino in one and in the other, the pièce de résistance; the true reason for this entire project.

Their own full service, BDSM kink club.

He already had the name picked out, and as majority shareholder, he was exercising his rights on that point. Luckily, they'd all agreed.

Iniquity.

All ten of them were in the lifestyle. That had been a must when he'd started putting together the concept for this resort, even if the other shareholders hadn't echoed the sentiment. All the investors needed to understand the intricacies of kink to make this work without any dissent from people who didn't understand the mechanics of their particular brand of predilection. That had meant it had taken a little longer to construct an investment team with both the finances and the drive to be a part of this, but it had been worth it to amass the right kind of people. And more importantly, he was happy with the team.

Ho looked across at them all and wondered what they were thinking. Whether they were trying to visualise the plans he'd shown them now they were in situ.

They all had their own stories. There was a reason why each of them was ready to buy into his concept right now.

Ryan and Zoe had complete faith in him. They weren't as wealthy as the rest of the investors and had contributed one million to the purchase between the two of them. Neither of them knew that Luca himself had contributed the additional million dollars needed and put that in Zoe's name, so they actually had a whole share each, rather than half. He knew they would have argued otherwise, but this was his gift to them. They'd allowed him into the life they'd shared for almost twenty years and given him the family he'd been searching for. That was more than any amount of money could buy.

His cousin, Dani, was getting more and more irritated with her current situation and his father constantly overlooking her abilities. His father was a brilliant businessman, but he was old school when it came to gender equality. One day, it would bite him in the ass.

Ash Millington was a stockbroker whiz kid who had recently lost his way after the death of his wife and child.

The man had come to him privately and asked to stay here on site and project manage the operation.

Luca hadn't been sure at first. He liked Ash well enough, but the guy was a suit; used to wheeling and dealing in the hustle and bustle of the stock exchange.

It had only been much later that Luca had appreciated that his talent for wheeling and dealing could be transposed into organising the huge undertaking to get this resort configured from the ground up. Ash had proved himself before they even made it this far. Getting together proposal, bids and estimates, then vetting each company before presenting the information to him. Luca couldn't deny that his work was sound and organised.

Of course, there was another very real motivation for Luca to agree. This project was his baby and the top project managers, the people he would trust to handle a development of this scale, didn't want to be holed up on an uninhabited island with no electricity and where the only fresh water came straight from a stream. And they were in enough demand that they didn't need the financial incentive.

Sure, the guy was running like the devil was on his heels, but perhaps the distraction of this project would bring him some closure.

Next to Ash stood Kayla and Marcus Thorne - members of the staid British aristocracy. They were siblings of inherited wealth with close familial links to the royal family, so they desperately wanted a private venue to practice their kink where they wouldn't be recognised. Luca figured they had a scare or two which had given them some impetus.

They were cautious though, buying in a half share, each with the option to upgrade to a full share. He was confident that would be sooner rather than later.

Dallas Johnson was a pro golf player who knew his career was coming to its natural end and was looking to the future. The scandal he'd recently been involved in meant he was more than ready for something new. He had already agreed to being a resident golf coach for the resort, another string to their bow, and a great source of additional income.

Kink alone wasn't going to float this investment. He'd always known that, but it had been crystallised for him after some in-depth conversations with another of the investors.

That's why there were going to be two hotels: two separate halves to the island.

One half would be purely vanilla and kept separated from the other half. Not that there weren't plenty of BDSM practitioners who'd be keen to get on the golf course when they weren't scening in the dungeon. Or prevail themselves of the health spa or the water sports – the type that took place on actual water, rather than in the club.

The entertainment and activities on the island would be inclusive. It was only after dark, when their wicked sides came out to play, that there'd be any difference.

But they needed the income generated from a regular, adults only, resort which offered luxury facilities and a few of the bonuses which came from being situated on a private island.

Kink and the opportunity to be a live sex venue was just one of them. Gambling was another.

Not that private islands were exempt from regulation. But it was a damn sight easier to get special licensing when there was nobody local to complain.

There were two final investors that made up their numbers. Saul Stephens was a playboy bachelor, always looking for his next adventure. But he had his secrets and Luca was one of the few who were privy to them. He also had more money than Midas.

That just left Zack Kincaid. He was the quiet type and had already made it clear he would be a silent investor. It was actually Dani who had enlisted him in a roundabout way, so Luca didn't know him as well as the others, but he was a good fit. Zack was an investment broker, so this was right up his street.

It was also his expertise which had helped Luca evolve the plans for the resort. The man had an incredible talent for knowing what made a sound investment. Luca had expanded the blueprint for the island in accordance with Zack's observations and knew the project would be more successful as a result.

Initially, he'd wondered if there was a relationship between Zack and Dani. Looking at them now, and the indifferent way they interacted, it was difficult to imagine there was anything between them. So he guessed it was purely professional and Zack just brokered some of Dani's investments.

While Zack was quiet and withdrawn, Dani was bubbly and effusive, chattering away. Right now, she had her sales pitch going, even though it wasn't needed because she was preaching to the choir. But if it helped the others process their vision, then all the better.

He hoped they could see what he saw, because this little diamond in the rough was going to be magnificent after they'd polished it up.

The ten of them were about to become the masters of paradise.

In more ways than one.

Luca Moreno,
Ryan and Zoe Moore

Chapter One

Zoe Moore stretched out on the sun lounger at the all-inclusive, luxury resort her husband had brought her to, and took a sip of the cocktail he handed her. Its graduating, ombre tones mirrored the colour of the sunset they had enjoyed the evening before as they'd strolled hand in hand along the beach. The colours here were so vivid and dazzling. From the white sandy beaches to the striking turquoise waters to the lush greenery painted with bold splashes of exotic red and yellow flowers. So different from the dull, dreary weather back home in the UK. The air was perfumed with hibiscus. The sea breeze warm and inviting with a hint of fresh ocean.

From her vantage point here near the poolside bar, she could still enjoy the ebb and flow of the surf which was just a short walk away.

When Ryan, her husband of almost two decades, settled back down next to her, she flipped onto her front.

"Can you put some sunscreen on my back please?" she asked, looking at him over her shoulder.

"Sure, babe," he said with a suggestive wink as he picked

up the bottle of lotion. He undid her bikini top, and Zoe held it in place with one hand as she continued to sip on her drink through the straw.

His strong hands soothed her as he slathered the coconut fragranced liquid over her skin. She had a nice glow, but burned easily, so always took care to protect herself.

Her gaze wandered lazily over the other resort patrons. The singles, watching and prowling. The couples, touching, laughing, comfortable together. The beautiful people, confident in their perfection, soaking up the admiration of others.

That's when she saw him.

He was definitely one of the beautiful people with his glossy, black hair cut short but longer on top showing a slight curl, his deeply tanned skin and impressive six pack abs. He had an exotic, foreign look about him, but not local. Mediterranean, maybe. He'd been swimming and water droplets caressed his body in a way she expected many of the young women who were eying hungrily might like to. Even happily married, she could admit the desire of wanting to trace some of that tempting drizzle with her tongue.

She couldn't yet decide whether he was single, but she very much doubted it. No way a man that looked like him was going to be holidaying solo. She looked around and made a game out of trying to work out which lucky woman was his other half.

"See something you like?" Ryan whispered in her ear as he dipped his hands suggestively down the outer sides of her breasts.

Zoe blushed and sucked in a breath. Busted!

She dragged her gaze away and looked at Ryan, whose face was right next to hers. She gave him a wicked grin. "Well, you can't deny that guy is hawt!" She closed the gap between them and dropped a quick kiss on his full lips. "Almost as hot as you."

It was true. Ryan was equally ripped, though he looked entirely different with his tousled, longish hair with natural sun kissed streaks. Zoe would be lying if she said she was oblivious to the many appreciative looks her husband also received. He was one of the beautiful people, too.

His eyes crinkled into an indulgent smile and he winked before pulling her in for a longer, deeper kiss which made her toes curl.

"Hmm," he murmured when he finally pulled away. "I don't know, I think maybe someone's heading the right way for a spanking."

Desire skittered down Zoe's spine and goose bumps popped out on her flesh despite the intense heat of the sun. Maybe it was time to blow this joint and pursue some adult fun back at their cabana. She moved to reach for him, but he eluded her.

"Uh-uh. Naughty little girls have to wait for their pleasure," he teased before adjusting his obviously swelling cock in his trunks and turning to dive into the cool water of the pool.

Zoe pretend pouted as she refastened the clasp of her bikini, but when she sat up, she found the hot guy looking at her. Had he been watching their little display? The thought sent shiver of awareness skittering through her and she forced herself to look away.

* * *

Ryan Moore approached the bar later that day and took a vacant stool while he waited for the busy bar tender to get to him. He wasn't in any hurry. He was here for a well-earned rest and some quality time with his wife. Ten days of relaxation; sun, surf, and sex. They'd both been working too hard recently.

He swivelled around, his back to the bar, and looked out

over the adults only resort with its laid-back atmosphere and top-notch facilities with a smile. A random group had congregated on the beach for a game of volleyball and the low buzz of jet skis hummed at the mouth of the bay. They were on the list of things he wanted to do, along with scuba diving, a trip on the glass bottomed boat to watch the sea life and swimming with the dolphins. For now, though, he was content just to unwind and decompress and catch some rays.

Someone walked up to the bar next to him and Ryan recognised him as the guy who had caught Zoe's eye earlier. He smiled and nodded his head in greeting and the guy returned the gesture and took the stool next to him.

When he perused the bar and realised the wait, he swung his seat around like Ryan.

Ryan looked at him and nodded at the jet skis in the bay. "Really fancy having a go at that," he said conversationally. "Have you tried it?"

"Oh, yes!" the guy replied with a hint of an accent; Italian, Ryan guessed. "It's a real blast."

"I'll have to get me and Zoe signed up. There's a whole bunch of stuff I want to try. I hope she's up for it too."

"Your girlfriend?" he asked, nodding over to where Zoe was stretched out, her superb curves on display.

"My wife," Ryan told him, following his appreciative gaze with an indulgent smile. "We're celebrating our nineteenth wedding anniversary."

The guy looked at him with a raised eyebrow. "You're a lucky man to have found something that enduring, but seriously, you don't look old enough to have been married that long, either of you."

Ryan chuckled. "We started young, idiot teens that we were, but I don't regret a day." He didn't admit to the eighteen-year-old twins they had just waved off to university. At thirty-six he *did* feel too young to have both an adult son and daughter, but Zoe had fallen pregnant before they'd finished school; careless kids that they'd been back then. Still, they'd made the most of it, struggled for a while, supported each other through further education as teenage parents and been all the more grateful for their achievements and successes.

Zoe had been right behind him when he wanted to risk everything to start his own business. She'd never doubted him at all. She'd stepped in as secretary, telephonist, form filler, researcher, coffee maker, and general jack of all trades... or maybe he should say 'Jill' of all trades. She'd cheerfully looked after the kids, the house, as well as juggled a job, and put food on the table while he worked ridiculously long hours to get that business established.

Ryan was well aware that he owed his success as much to her as he did to his own inspiration and hard work. Now that they were reaping the benefits and had achieved a comfortable level of wealth, he wanted nothing more than to reward her for the faith she'd had in him.

He wanted to give her more.

He wanted to give her the world.

In fact, his mind was already turning over the possibility of granting what he believed was one her most guarded, unspoken desires. One that he found rather tantalising himself.

Sticking out his hand, he introduced himself properly to the guy sitting next to him. "I'm Ryan. How long are you here for?"

Chapter Two

"Pleased to meet you, I'm Luca." Luca Moreno shook hands with the dude who had struck up a conversation with him. He was pleased to have some male company if he was honest. These 'mystery shopper' trips that his father insisted on for the family chain of resorts could get tedious as a singleton if you didn't connect with the right people.

Not for the first time, Luca wished he had a 'significant other' to share some of this with, but the truth was, he could never be sure if anyone he hooked up with was just after his money. Conversely, that was one of the benefits of these incognito trips. No one knew who he was, so their responses were far more genuine. Not that he was ever at a loss for company. There were always plenty of women willing to throw themselves at him, but even that had become tedious over the last few years.

Since he'd hit thirty, he realised he wanted more. He found himself envious of the commitments and constancy people like Ryan had.

Still, it wasn't the norm for him to be approached by part

of a couple. Generally, those of that ilk were too wrapped up in themselves to look beyond their own little bubble unless it was to socialise with likeminded couples because of the obvious proverbial fifth wheel scenario.

Maybe Ryan was looking for someone to accompany him on the events he had mentioned in case his wife wasn't interested. Well, that worked for him, since he was planning to check them all out as part of his job. It was good to experience things through a genuine customer's eyes.

"I arrived a couple of days ago and I'm booked for a fortnight. Did you just get here?" Luca mentioned.

Ryan nodded. "Yesterday. Haven't had a chance to look around properly yet. We just wanted to relax and unwind initially, but it looks like there's some great entertainment."

"Well, if you need any recommendations, this isn't my first trip, so I know the place pretty well." And wasn't that an understatement.

"Cool," Ryan replied. "It's a bit overwhelming knowing what to do first. I mean the online details outlined all the activities, but I haven't seen a leaflet or anything that tells me about it all now I'm here."

Luca frowned. That was something he'd have to look into. "No problem, man. I'm happy to help."

The bar tender finally got around to serving them and since Luca was busy making a mental note that they needed to increase the bar staff he was unprepared for Ryan's next question.

"Hey, Luca, if you're not busy right now, maybe you could come and chat with Zoe and I about what's popular and the best time to do those things?"

He looked around with a frown. "Unless you're here with someone, of course, and I'm interrupting. In which case, forget I asked."

Luca shrugged. "No, I'm flying solo for this trip," he

replied. He looked over at Ryan's wife. She'd caught his eye earlier with her lush curves that went on for days, a far cry from the usual stick figures he saw strutting around. Why not? It certainly wasn't any hardship to spend a couple of hours with a friendly guy and a beautiful woman.

* * *

Zoe peered at Ryan over the top of her sunglasses as he began walking back over to her with the hot guy in tow.

Suddenly she felt subconscious. It wasn't that she was embarrassed by her rather more voluptuous figure; on the contrary, she loved her curves and, more importantly, so did Ryan. But as the two of them grew closer she was uncomfortably aware that she was a far cry from all the model thin young girls who'd been trying to catch his attention.

Then she laughed at herself. What the heck did she care anyway? She wasn't out to impress anyone.

She immediately relaxed, the amusement still showing on her face and spreading into an easy smile as Ryan introduced them.

"Luca, this is my wife, Zoe. Zoe, Luca's offered to give us the benefit of his knowledge and experience with the activities."

She leaned forward and extended her hand. "Pleased to meet you, Luca."

The thrill that ran down her arm when he enclosed her fingers in his firm grip was a surprise. In almost twenty years of marriage, she'd never been tempted by another man. That wasn't to say she didn't appreciate a good-looking guy. She was married, not dead, after all. But neither had she had such a visceral reaction to anyone other than her husband before.

Zoe played it cool and resisted the urge to yank her hand

away, but she was nevertheless glad for the obscurity of the sunglasses.

Her nipples, of course, were an entirely different matter. It was out of her control to stop them pebbling beneath the flimsy material of her swimsuit. Embarrassed, she leaned forward and grabbed her drink, praying Ryan didn't notice. No matter how her wayward body reacted, she would never consciously disrespect him in such a way, and she was appalled at her body for betraying her.

Doing her best to change the direction of her treacherous thoughts, Zoe gestured to Ryan's lounger. "Have a seat, Luca," she offered. "Ryan and I can share."

She shuffled forwards so her husband could squeeze in behind her and lay back against his chest within the vee of his legs.

As they all settled and the conversation switched to an innocuous discussion of the merits of different activities, Ryan snaked his arm around her waist.

Zoe thought nothing of it at first, but then he started stroking his fingers across the gentle swell of her belly, occasionally dipping dangerously close to the forbidden territory covered by her low-rise bikini bottoms. Well, forbidden in public, anyway.

Zoe bit her lip and tried to keep her breathing even as heat streaked through her veins and goosebumps sprang up along her sensitised skin everywhere his fingers roamed.

His other arm joined in the sensual teasing, his knuckle skimming the sensitive skin at the side of her neck before curving around and lazily tracing the upper curve of her ample breasts.

Arousal bloomed, firing a reluctant desire. There was no hiding the way her nipples strained in reaction this time. They formed hard, round buds which pressed starkly against the snug fabric, but at least it was Ryan who sparked the response.

Her breathing had become erratic under his covert assault and she struggled to keep it even while ruthlessly stifling the urge to writhe against the growing bulge she could feel digging into her back.

She swallowed and took a long pull at her drink. What on earth had gotten into Ryan to be toying with her like this in front of another man.

Worse, a glance at Luca proved his eyes were following the path of Ryan's hands, and a quick glimpse over her shoulder revealed her husband watching Luca, watching them.

She and Ryan enjoyed a pretty inventive and often kinky sex life, but although it appeared innocuous, this was something else.

What the heck was he playing at?

Chapter Three

Z oe shouldn't have been surprised when Ryan asked Luca to join them for dinner that evening. They had chatted the afternoon away, discussed everything the resort had to offer, on which Luca seemed unusually knowledgeable, and then moved on to the lesser-known attractions of the tropical island paradise.

There was an easy camaraderie between the two men. In fact, they seemed so comfortable with each other you'd be forgiven for thinking they'd known each other for years.

She was more surprised that Luca accepted Ryan's invitation to dinner, although to begin with he demurred. "As generous as the offer is, Ryan, I'm sure you don't really want a spare interrupting a romantic dinner for two.

"Nonsense; we don't mind entertaining a third, do we, hun?" Ryan looked at her with a raised eyebrow.

Was it her own overactive imagination or did that question seemed to be loaded?

"Of course not," she replied with a smile.

Luca looked torn and Ryan pushed the advantage. "Come on, Luca, you can't tell me you'd prefer to eat alone. Or do you have some beach babe lined up?" he asked with a wink, giving Luca the perfect out if he was really set against joining them.

Luca laughed. "No beach babes. I just don't want to cramp your style," he said easily.

"Then it's settled," Ryan decided, refusing to take no for an answer.

He snagged one of the booths when they entered the dining room, and somehow Zoe found herself sandwiched between two hot men. She was also pretty certain she was getting quite a few death glares from some of the single women who were on the prowl.

Throughout dinner, Ryan kept up his quiet assault of her senses. His work roughened fingers pushed the hem of her light, summer dress up her thighs. The rasp of his calloused hands against her skin sent ripples of soft arousal undulating through her body. The sustained offensive built slowly but surely into a much bigger wave and her desire notched higher and higher but had no ready outlet, leaving her desperate and frustrated in the best possible way. She'd given up wondering what he was trying to achieve. Sex games were nothing new in their life, but unfortunately having adult kids in the house and the pace of their busy jobs meant it had been a long time since they'd been able to indulge themselves fully, even in something as seemingly innocuous as touching.

Brushing.

Stroking.

Caressing.

Somehow the fact that he did it all in public with another guy sat next to them, even if her legs were covered by the table-cloth, made it all the more titillating. Occasionally his fingers would strum across her lace covered mound, making her hot and wet and needy. And throughout it all he managed to keep up an animated conversation with Luca.

If the other man noticed her distraction - or her dilemma - he was too polite to mention it.

They decided to take a break before ordering dessert. Personally, Zoe couldn't wait to get back to the privacy of their cabana for an altogether different kind of dessert, but Ryan had insisted.

Dratted man was intent on keeping her wound up and unfulfilled.

She looked out over the nearby dance floor and, on a whim, decided to try and divert her craving.

"Come and dance with me," she asked Ryan, pulling at his arm.

Ryan looked at the slow dancing couples plastered together on the darkened patio with its atmospheric fairy lights. "Actually, I was about to go to the bar and get another round of drinks, but I'm sure Luca wouldn't mind dancing with you."

Zoe's mouth fell open in surprise as Ryan pulled her out of the booth with him and looked expectantly and Luca.

Zoe looked down at her feet in embarrassment. "Don't worry, it's fine," she mumbled, worrying her fingers.

"On the contrary, it would be my pleasure," Luca assured her, his lilting accent licking at her already aroused senses. This wasn't a good idea. Why was Ryan throwing them together like this?

"Have fun," her husband said patting her backside before turning towards the bar with a wicked wink.

Zoe lifted her eyes to Luca. Damn the man was sexy! "Honestly, you don't need to..."

"I know," he interrupted. "But actually, it's been a long time since I danced with a beautiful woman."

Zoe laughed. His words were so ridiculous that they shattered the awkwardness she felt, at least.

"It's true," Luca insisted as he followed her outside, his

hand burning against the small of her back. "Usually, my encounters tend more towards tearing up the sheets and wondering how much of a battering my credit card is going to take. Social niceties like dancing are a rare luxury."

"I'm not entirely sure I believe you," Zoe retorted with a smile and a shake of her head as he pulled her into his arms. "I'm certain any of the single women here would be more than happy to dance with you."

Luca gave her a lopsided grin which kicked up one side of his tantalisingly full lips. "Maybe so, but all the while their concentration would be on moving things to the next level and how quickly they could do that. Believe me, I speak from experience. With you, I can relax and just enjoy the moment, because I know there's no ulterior motive."

Zoe didn't know what to say to that, so she said nothing.

Luca settled his cheek against her forehead, and they settled into a comfortable silence. They swayed slowly together to the lazy rhythm of the music. She could feel the bulge of his cock pressing against the softness of her stomach and was hyper aware of the heat of his hand burning into her hip, but since it was vastly inappropriate, she didn't mention that either.

She stuck it out for one dance which had done absolutely nothing to cool her raging libido. When she returned to their table she instantly gulped down the fruity cocktail Ryan handed her, but the liquid did little to ease the kind of thirst she was feeling either.

She wasn't close to being drunk, but she was pleasantly buzzed, so the comments she caught from a couple of girls close by, took her unawares and completely sideswiped her.

"God! Can you believe that fat cow monopolising all the hot guys?"

At first, she wasn't even aware they were talking about her, but as realisation dawned, Zoe's spine went rigid, and she felt an angry heat prickle her neck as a mixture of rage and embarrassment rushed through her.

"Don't be stupid," someone else said. "Two good looking guys like them wouldn't see anything in someone that old and chunky. They're obviously just being polite. I bet they can't wait for her to fuck off."

Her chest tightened painfully, and she fisted her hands at her sides. She knew she had curves, but she'd never considered herself fat. Or old. Jeez, she was only thirty-six!

Looking at them from the corner of her eye, she realised the pair who were openly ogling and fluttering their coy looks and eyelashes at her husband and Luca were barely any older than her eighteen-year-old daughter. Gross! Did they really think these men were cradle snatchers? The idea made her feel sick to her stomach. Was this the sort of thing poor Luca normally had to deal with?

A couple more rude and lewd comments and she decided she'd had enough. She spun around, more than ready to leave. Instead, she found herself nose to chest with Ryan. He pulled her body, which was now quivering with rage and indignity, to him and placed a finger on her lips.

"Hey, baby. Just ignore them. They're not worth getting upset or spoiling our evening for."

Zoe sucked in a ragged breath, but let him soothe her for a few, brief moments. "Well, I'm afraid it's a bit late for that," she told him self-consciously, realising they'd already attracted some watchers. "Let's just get out of here." She blinked back some stupid tears and tried to pull out of his arms, but Ryan held her tight and kissed her forehead.

Then, to her surprise, she heard Luca's voice cutting through the muted buzz of the room. "I don't think my friend appreciates you speaking about his *wife* in that way."

"That's okay, we can still show both of you a good time," said one with a clearly drunken giggle.

"Oh my Gawd! He's *married* to the chubby bitch. What's wrong with him?" said the other.

Zoe bristled with anger.

"You're right, let's get out of here," Ryan agreed, kissing the top of her head and giving her a supportive squeeze.

As they turned away and headed towards the door, she couldn't help a satisfied smile as she heard Luca say, "You girls might think you have beautiful figures, but your attitude makes you ugly."

It might not have been the ending she'd expected of the evening, but it made her feel better.

Chapter Four

As it turned out, it wasn't the end of the evening after all.

A few minutes later Luca caught up with them. "I'm so sorry about that," he said sincerely to both her and Ryan.

Zoe gave him a small smile. "Why are you apologising?" she asked. "It wasn't your fault."

Luca just shrugged in that expressive, Italian fashion. "Well, I picked up some Champagne from the bar for you," he said, offering the bottle to Ryan. "It's not fair that your night was cut short like that."

"Yours either," Ryan replied. "So at least have a drink with us since you went to the bother of buying it, and let's finish the evening off on a happier note."

Zoe stayed quiet, a little pensive, on the walk back to their secluded cabana. But as the three of them climbed the steps to the luxury chalet on stilts at the edge of a peaceful sea with the tropical forest with its chorus of unfamiliar bird calls at its back, she turned to Luca. "Thank you for sticking up for me.

We've only just met; you didn't have to get yourself stuck in the middle of my drama."

"And what sort of person would I be, if I allowed people to talk to my new friends in such a manner?" he replied lightly, and she expected him to turn away. Instead, his beautiful, melted chocolate eyes clung intensely to hers for a long moment. "They're only jealous, you know that, don't you? Don't ever let people like that undermine you, because you're beautiful just the way you are." He ran a knuckle down her cheek and at the very same moment, Ryan leaned in. "Truth," he agreed as he pressed a glass of champagne into her hand and kissed her other cheek.

The energy of feeling them both touching her at the same time made her breath hitch and suddenly she wasn't thinking about mean girls anymore.

* * *

Ryan was angry. How dare some snotty kid, barely old enough to drink, speak about his Zoe like that? Within hearing range, too! Never mind that it had killed the mood he'd been building all evening.

Although he'd chosen to get Zoe out there and walk away, he had a new level of respect for Luca for defending her the way he had. It hadn't been his fight.

Now they were back in the privacy of their cabana, Ryan just wanted to take her mind off it. He had a plan; he just hoped Zoe wasn't too self-conscious after what had happened. She didn't really have any body image issues, but as the father of a teenage daughter, Ryan knew only too well how a well-timed slur could leave its mark.

Now he just needed to execute his plan in such a manner that there was an easy out for both Luca and Zoe, without things being awkward, if his judgement was wrong and neither of them were on board.

He pulled her down next to him on the couch and slipped an arm around her waist while Luca took the chair opposite.

After enough small talk and champagne to relax them all again, Ryan turned his attention to his wife. "I think it's time for your punishment, don't you?" he said casually, though he was anything but.

Zoe started and look at him and out of the corner of his eye he saw Luca raised an amused eyebrow.

"Wh-what?" Zoe stuttered, her head swivelling around in surprise. "Pardon?" She asked again as if she hadn't heard properly the first time.

"You earned yourself a spanking earlier, remember?"

This time she choked on her drink, so Ryan smoothly removed the glass from her hand and leaned over to place it on the side table. He used the same momentum to tug her over his knee with the arm that was around her waist.

"Ryan?" Zoe questioned him, but there was a breathless catch to her voice. After damn near twenty years he could read her well, and knew it meant she was turned on.

"Did you forget, my sweet?" he asked, ready to backtrack if she argued against it.

"No," she whispered, throwing a cautious glance at Luca, then back at him before she gave him her submission and lay limply across his lap.

"You don't mind if I discipline my wife, do you, Luca?" he asked the other man, noting the way his gaze was pinned to the place where Ryan's hand was rubbing circles on Zoe's luscious backside. "It's a dynamic we enjoy playing out, but I'll understand if it makes you uncomfortable."

"Far be it for me to criticise other people's kink," Luca replied. "You've made me more than welcome, all day, I certainly don't want to disrupt your normal process."

Ryan nodded his head in acknowledgement as he smoothed his hand along the back of Zoe's thigh, pushing the fabric of the dress up and out of the way at the same time until he'd bared her.

He could feel the laboured rise and fall of her chest where her breasts pressed against his outer thigh, the stiff peaks of her nipples drilling into him. He smoothed his hands across the swell of her ass and made sure her dress was tucked out of the way before he pinned her legs between his own. Then he used the hold to keep her in place while he used both hands to peel back her lacy underwear down to her knees. He left them there, knowing the psychology of being bound by them in plain sight like that was far more powerful than if he removed them completely.

Ryan rubbed and squeezed each of Zoe's bared buttocks to warm them for the spanking and flicked a glance at Luca. The other man's eyes were glued firmly to Zoe's backside, and he drew his tongue across his bottom lip.

Ryan hid a smile and brought his hand down, hard, over first one buttock and then the other in quick succession. Zoe yelped, her body flinched instinctively, as she always did with the first spank.

He paused for long enough to admire the twin handprints blooming over her cheeks.

"I caught my wife eying up another man," he said conversationally to Luca as if there was nothing at all unusual going on. "So, I'm sure you agree that she deserves a good spanking for her actions."

Ryan settled into a steady rhythm and Zoe relaxed against him, the small noises that erupted from her lips taking on a heavier, more guttural tone.

After a few minutes, he stopped and rubbed the fleshly globes that had turned a pretty rose blush under his hand.

"Of course," he said, raising his eyes to Luca. "Since you

were the guy she was ogling, maybe you'd like to participate in her punishment?"

Luca raised his eye slowly to Ryan's and for a moment the two men just looked at each other in silent communication.

Across his knee, Zoe let out a gasping croak, but she didn't utter a word of dissent.

Ryan raised one eyebrow and gave Luca the out. "Unless you're not the spanking kind, of course."

"On the contrary," Luca replied, his voice full of gravel. "I would be honoured to help discipline such a naughty little girl."

A smile spread across Ryan's face at his choice of words. Oh yes, his instinct had been spot on. This was a man who was not a stranger to a bit of kink himself.

* * *

Luca almost wanted to pinch himself to see if he was dreaming because the times when a hot guy invited him to spank his equally hot wife only took place inside his fantasies. But if this was a dream, then he sure as hell didn't want to interrupt it right now. Better to get to the good stuff before he had to wake up.

Zoe was the picture of beautiful submission. She was draped, limply, over Ryan's knees, her lush backside a pleasing shade of rose. She was everything he wanted in a woman. Then again, Ryan was everything he wanted in a man too. Hair long enough to get a grip on, a strong muscled body and a dominant personality.

For a moment Luca knew a stab of envy that these two had each other, but he pushed it ruthlessly aside. He'd been invited to share in a brief moment out of time and he'd treasure it for what it was, knowing how rare this gift was; his perfect rolled into a single delicious package.

He refused to spoil it by brooding over something he knew he'd never find for himself.

He was a bisexual switch, and he loved all kinds of kink, both the giving and the receiving. He was pretty certain that Ryan was completely straight, and probably not even bi-curious. Why would he be when he had a woman like Zoe at his fingertips and a relationship enduring enough for them to have explored and refined all the things they enjoyed together?

Luca wasn't greedy; he'd happily settle for one or the other if he found someone who matched his desires but so far no one had even come close. Right now, he was being offered a slice of heaven and he was damn well going to grab on with both hands and revel in every single moment he was gifted with, instead of wasting time yearning for more.

Joining the couple across the room, he dropped to his knees opposite them, waiting for Ryan's permission before he put his hands on Zoe. Even that small thing lit a fire within him that outweighed the simplicity of the gesture.

He placed his tanned hand against the pink of her scorching skin and admired the contrast as much as he absorbed the heat. Closing his eyes, he committed the moment to memory.

And then he brought his hand down with a stinging slap against her left cheek and appreciated the pliancy of her flesh as it rippled, the huffing gasp that greeted his discipline. His cock hardened impossibly.

Over and over his hand bounced against Zoe's backside while Ryan held her. The sounds she made! The mewling and yelping were the musical backdrop to their little soiree. When he judged she'd had enough he cupped her burning cheeks in his palm and held the heat against her skin.

Against his skin.

Ryan mirrored his movements and together they both rubbed away the sting.

Luca instinctively made to check on Zoe, then stopped himself and looked to Ryan for askance. The nod he received was a benefaction and Luca grasped Zoe by the hair and lifted her head to see her face. She looked back at him with tear drenched blue eyes and she had never looked so beautiful. He cupped her cheek and brushed the tears away with his thumb.

"You are truly beautiful in your punishment," he told her reverently.

Her lips parted and her chest heaved, her breath fanning him, and Luca wanted nothing more than to kiss her.

But she wasn't his and that really would be overstepping.

Except Ryan knew. The man's intuition was remarkable. "I think Zoe would appreciate it, if you kissed her better."

He said it quietly, but the words exploded loudly in Luca's head.

Zoe made a small, mewling sound and lifted her torso, so she was closer to him. Behind them both, Ryan picked her up and bodily moved her, removing her underwear and arranging her on his lap with her back to his chest and her knees hooked over his own. Then he splayed them wide so Luca could manoeuvre into the vee their spread legs provided.

Ryan threw him an intense look before he gripped Zoe by the hair and held her there for Luca. A needy moan issued from Zoe's parted lips, her eyes beseeched him, and Luca swallowed the sound as he took her mouth and thrust his tongue into her welcoming depths.

* * *

Zoe was almost sobbing into Luca's mouth. She couldn't remember being this turned on - or this frustrated - in her entire life, and Ryan was pretty good at heaping on the torment when he wanted. But the opportunities for full blown kink had been few and far between as the twins turned into young adults and this was taking things to an entirely new level.

Now she was so wet and horny that the smell of her arousal wafted through the air between the three of them like some raging pheromone.

There were too many clothes between them all and she was desperate to remove some of them, but she wasn't sure how far Ryan wanted to take this scene. Inviting another man to spank her and kiss her better was one thing. The carnal images in Zoe's head were quite another. She wanted more.

He answered the question for her. The benefit of years of intimacy and knowing exactly how to read her. Untying the ribbon of the halter at the back of her neck, Ryan pushed down the stretchy, ruched bodice of her sundress and bared her breasts. The fabric grazed against her nipples and she welcomed the sensation before his hands replaced it. He cupped and plucked and the stiff, aching tips while Luca fisted his hands into her hair, now Ryan had released it, and continued his passionate assault on her mouth.

Ryan's hand slipped down to where her dress was still bunched around her waist. He didn't hang around, just plunged two fingers into her wet, needy core.

Zoe cried out in pleasure and Luca captured the sound before nipping at her lower lip and tightening his fingers deliciously against her scalp.

She writhed against Ryan's plunging fingers; it was impossible to stop herself. Instead, she fumbled with the buttons on Luca's shirt.

She wanted skin.

She wanted to feel the heat of these two bodies surrounding her.

Stroking her.

Punishing her.
Fucking her.
Taking her in any way they pleased.
Together.

Chapter Five

"Taste her, Luca," Ryan invited, when they finally broke the kiss to drag in some much-needed air. He removed his fingers from her slick channel and sucked them into his mouth, his eyes on Luca's the entire time.

He stripped Zoe's dress over her head and leaned back against the sofa, taking her with him. Tweaking each of her nipples, then cupping her breasts and squeezing them together, he offered them to Luca like a prize.

Luca dipped his head and pulled one of the budded peaks into his mouth. Zoe groaned and thrust her chest out, urging him on. Silently begging him for more.

He nipped and suckled, taking his fill while Ryan held her firmly in place, his hands like bands around the fullness of her flesh and the whole thing was wildly erotic.

Ryan's erection dug into Zoe's back and she wiggled suggestively against him, but his only reaction was to squeeze her breasts tighter.

Luca looked at Ryan for direction and he gave a brief nod. The permission given, Luca trailed his mouth down Zoe's skin, kissing and licking his way across the feminine swell of her abdomen to her delightfully bare mons.

He dawdled a while, running his fingers oh-so-lightly along the length of her thighs, blowing on the sensitised skin of her labia, but never giving Zoe what she really craved.

Ryan's arm banded around Zoe's waist, stilling her wriggling and stopping her from doing anything but waiting, anticipating, yearning for Luca's touch.

His hands.

His mouth.

His tongue.

Anything.

He plucked indolently at her nipples with his other hand, first one, then the other, ramping up her need until she was panting and begging.

Finally...finally Luca swept his tongue along her seam and she whimpered in gratitude, undulating her pelvis as much as Ryan's hold would allow.

"I think we'll need to tie you down, next time, to stop you wriggling," Ryan murmured and the image he provoked had her pussy gushing in response.

"Oh, she likes that idea!" Luca chuckled, squeezing her thighs and lapping up her cream with the broad of his tongue.

"Next time, sweetheart. Next time," Ryan promised and the fact that he implied the three of them might do this all over again had Zoe keening in delight.

"Yes! Oh yes, please...please..." Zoe moaned.

Ryan shifted her slightly, slipping his arms underneath hers so he could play with both of her nipples.

"Put your arms behind your back and keep them there, or everything stops," he ordered.

* * *

Zoe scrambled to obey, she was desperate to come and so very close. She wasn't about to do anything to lose that reward. But she could just about manage the buttons on Ryan's fly. It took a bit of fumbling, but she finally had him freed. He pulled her tight against him in response, wedging her arms between them, but she could still reach behind his ball sac and massage his perineum. She knew how it drove him wild and greeted his muffled groan and subsequent curses with a satisfied smile.

His response was to pull and pinch her nipples and that slight edge of pleasure/pain had her crying out and flinging her head back on his shoulder. He maximised her response by grazing his teeth along her bared throat then biting down on the erogenous zone where her neck met her shoulder.

Luca took his cue and joined in the delicious assault on her senses, concentrating his efforts on her protruding clit which had poked out from behind its protective hood. He sucked it into his mouth and worried it with his tongue, manipulating it expertly until she was a mess of hungry need and desperate pleading.

The two of them played her perfectly, bringing her to the very edge of the peak but never allowing her to fall over. They took her there again and again, tantalising her with a climax only to steal it away at the last second.

"Beg," Ryan ordered.

Hell, what did they think she'd been doing all this time?

"Pl-please," she whimpered brokenly. "Please Ryan..." She panted between words. "Please Luca..." She arched and writhed madly within the constraints of their hands and mouths. "Please Sirs, let me come, I beg you. Please let me come. Pleeease."

"Good girl," Ryan breathed in her ear as he nodded to Luca.

Between her legs, Luca pressed his fingers inside her for the first time and teased her inner walls until he found her g-spot. He sucked her pouting clit into his mouth and suckled at it as Ryan twisted her nipples and Zoe exploded in an orgasm unlike any she'd known before.

The scream that erupted from her mouth was long and laboured and her body took on a life of its own, thrashing and bucking under the hands of these two impossibly perfect men.

Zoe panted hard and tried to regain her breath. Her hair was a wild tangle around her face and her entire body still tingled as Ryan moved her aside and started stripping off his clothes.

She didn't see the communication between them, but Luca did the same until they were both standing before her gloriously naked.

"Get on your knees," Ryan demanded, grabbing a fistful of hair and directing her head towards Luca's thick, straining cock. "It's our turn now."

Zoe scrambled to obey, she wanted nothing more than to give them a taste of the pleasure they'd just shown her. And the act of her husband's hand in her hair, guiding her to another man's cock, was so hot that her body started to catch fire all over again which she hadn't even considered possible after the strength of the orgasm she'd just experienced.

She licked the veiny underside of Luca's shaft before closing her lips around the head and swallowing him down. Ryan pushed her to take him deeper then manipulated her head, so her actions were not her own and he fucked her face with Luca's cock.

Zoe groped at Ryan's leg until she reached her husband's burgeoning member and clasped her fingers around it. She managed to set up a rhythmic pace between the two of them, until Luca also grabbed a handful of her hair, pulling her off of him and directing her to swap things around.

* * *

Luca looked down at Zoe as he pulled her mouth away from his own cock and fed her husband's to her. Fuck, this was the hottest thing he'd done in his life, and that was saying something. He looked at Ryan, who was watching Zoe take his cock compelled by Luca's hand.

Ryan chose that exact moment to look over at Luca and the lust that burned in his eyes was stark in its intensity. His gaze leisurely caressed Luca's body, down to where Zoe pumped his cock, then silently back up again, resting briefly on his mouth before returning to his eyes. Questions burned there and Luca's breath stuck in his chest for a long moment.

The vibes he was getting from Ryan were...shit, was he really going to do this? It might ruin everything.

Or it might make it one hundred percent perfect. *For you, anyway,* a little voice in the corner of his subconscious murmured.

Luca sighed, his eyes dropping to Ryan's lips then back to his face. Ryan stared back, his gaze intense, the desire which mirrored Luca's own reflected back at him. His cock jumped in response and a growl emanated from his lips as Zoe's hand wrapped firmly around his shaft, containing all that throbbing flesh while her mouth worked Ryan's pulsing member.

Ryan moved, just barely, leaning towards him ever so slightly, but it was enough.

Luca swooped in and crushed Ryan's mouth with his.

This...this was the stuff all his very deepest fantasies were made of, and for the first time in his life, he was living the dream.

* * *

Zoe felt the shift in the dynamic like it was a physical thing. Above her both men groaned softly and their fists in her hair tightened at the same time. But the forceful coercion to direct her actions was suddenly gone, as if something had distracted them.

Zoe angled her head and looked at them from beneath her lashes as she continued to suck and pump.

Her eyes widened and her groan of approval vibrated Ryan's length as she witnessed Luca kissing her husband with a passion that was clearly returned. They each had their free hand on the others nape and Zoe could hear the occasional sucking of lips as they devoured each other.

Damn, that was hot!

Chapter Six

Ryan didn't know what shocked him more. The fact that Luca had kissed him, or the fact that he'd enjoyed it. He'd only ever had eyes for Zoe. No matter that they'd been stupidly young, after her no one else had even registered.

Then there'd been kids and work; the business.

Life.

Things had only just slowed down long enough for them to take a breath. That's what this trip was about. A way to treat his wife, whose biggest indulgence until now had been books. Kinky books reflecting their varied sex life and particularly menage, which was her favourite.

That's what this had been born from. But while he'd found the idea titillating; the thought of choreographing the scene entirely at his own whim, a complete power trip, he'd never imagined things progressing along this particular tangent.

He'd believed the biggest obstacle might be jealousy. Had wondered if he might feel self-conscious baring his cock in front of another man. But holding his wife and watching another man eat her out at his own direction had been hot as fuck. A total turn on.

Luca kissing him; allowing that to happen, had completely blown his mind. And now he was wondering about the rest of it. But that's not what this was about. This was about Zoe. This was about giving her more.

Taking a step back from both of them, he resumed the mantle of control. "I think it's time to move this to the bedroom."

He didn't wait for their agreement, just helped Zoe up and pulled her along behind him, leaving Luca to follow... or not.

He knew what he wanted. The others needed to make their own choices.

Didn't mean he wasn't relieved when they both joined him. Not just Luca: he could walk away. But what he had engineered here could have repercussions for him and Zoe that might affect their life forever. They'd been together over twenty years, if you counted those young teen years where they'd fumbled through school before she'd become pregnant with the twins and things suddenly got real. All of that built a picture of the woman she was now, and he was pretty certain he could read her almost as well as himself. But there was always that 1% doubt.

Luca, on the other hand, was throwing out all kinds of mixed messages. Some dominant, some submissive, some straight... some not. And that was messing with his head a bit. But this wasn't the time to start second guessing things. That was a sure-fire recipe for disaster, so he did what he always did and took control. Of them both.

"Get on the bed, Luca," he ordered, throwing the other man a challenging look. "On your back."

Luca's mouth hitched ever so slightly on one side, in the smallest of half-smiles and he nodded almost imperceptibly before following the instruction.

Ryan felt the power of control surge through his body and harden him further. This was his show.

He pulled Zoe in front of him, her back against his chest, and looped his arm underneath her breasts. "Do you want him?" he murmured in her ear. He felt rather than heard the air leaving her lungs and then being sucked back in again.

"Yes," she breathed, laying her head against his shoulder while she stared down at Luca's prone form.

"Climb on then, sweetheart, and give him the ride of his life."

Zoe turned her head an looked at him and Ryan ducked his head and gave her a hard kiss followed by a swift swat to her backside that had her yelping and rushing to obey.

"I'll be right there," he promised. "I just need to get a few things."

He took a step back, waiting and watching as she straddled Luca. The other man helped her mount his jutting cock and Zoe cast her eyes from where he entered her, to Luca, and then back to Ryan as she sank slowly down on him.

Luca grabbed her by the waist and Ryan swallowed as he watched Zoe circle her hips then raise and lower herself, settling onto Luca's shaft. He gave them a satisfied smile before turning and heading for the bathroom. There were things he needed.

Grabbing lube and a pair of nipple clamps, Ryan returned. He looked at the two of them from the doorway of the en-suite for a moment before hurrying to join then, suddenly desperate to be part of the dynamic.

He smoothed his hand down Zoe's back. "Lean forward," he told her, tucking her long, red hair out of the way.

"Luca, suck on her nipples. Make them hard for me," he said, dangling the clover clamps with their attached chain from one of his fingers.

Luca cupped the generous mounds in his hands and went

to work while Ryan opened the bottle of lube and coated his fingers. Zoe's back arched and her rhythm faltered momentarily as he circled his finger around her puckered rosette, but as he delved further, she arched her spine, pushing her ass back to meet him in clear invitation.

He breached the tight ring of muscle with first one digit, then two, then scissored his fingers to ready her for penetration with something altogether bigger, Taking two cocks at the same time, one in each hole, would make her tight, and while they were no strangers to anal play, he needed to make sure she was properly prepared. She grunted a little at the pressure and writhed beneath his hand, but Luca gripped her thighs and held her still for him. Jeez, that was a turn on.

He added a third finger and heard her groan. She wasn't the only one. Ryan could feel Luca's cock through the thin membrane that separated them and felt it jump as he deliberately pressed his fingers down on the shaft before removing them and wiping his hands.

He tossed one of the nipple clamps to Luca as he pulled Zoe back up into a sitting position. "One each. Both at the same time."

They took a nipple each and Zoe panted shallowly as they both affixed the tight grips, allowing then to spring into place at the exact same moment.

She shrieked and panted, and Ryan pushed her forwards once more where Luca swallowed the sounds with a kiss.

He applied another generous squirt of lube, coated his cock liberally and made certain she was ready. As he lined himself up with her forbidden hole, he reached around and lifted the chain that attached the clamps. "Take this in your mouth, Luca," he demanded, holding it there and pushing it between the other man's lips when he opened. "Keep it there."

Luca's eye burned into him in their dark intensity, and he

jerked his head back, give the chain a sharp yank which had Zoe yelping and panting.

Ryan couldn't help the wide grin that spread across his face.

All humour was forgotten as he pushed forward into the confined space of Zoe's back hole. Luca eased out a little to give him room, but Zoe still whimpered at the pressure the two of them exerted.

Ryan stroked her back, murmuring to her gently. "It's okay babe, we'll take it slow," he soothed as he forced his way past the tight ring of muscle.

Amazingly, Luca was completely attuned to the pair of them. As Zoe held her breath and instinctively tensed against his entry, Luca manipulated he chain so that her breath left her in a gasp and she backed up against Ryan, letting him in another inch.

Ryan wound her long hair around his fist and forced her head back, then kissed the side of her bared throat and down her shoulder, encouraging her to relax. He was almost in.

"Oh god! It's too much," Zoe whimpered, her eyes screwed shut.

"Almost there sweetheart, he told her. "Just another inch."

Luca reached up a hand and cupped her cheek, stroking his thumb across her parched bottom lip. "You can do it, sweet Zoe," he encouraged. "You can take us both. That's what you want isn't it?"

"Yes," Zoe whispered on a breath. "More than anything."

Luca gave a nod and the chain pulled against her tender nubs once more, diverting her attention and Ryan took the opportunity to seat himself to the hilt.

They all breathed a sigh, every one of them. Then Ryan withdrew and Luca took his place.

They set up a slow, easy rhythm between them but too soon it wasn't enough, and the pace escalated.

Ryan was enflamed by both the feeling of Zoe's tight ring squeezing him and the stroke of Luca's cock against his own through the thin barrier of skin that separated them. Control spiralled away from him and he started pounding against the two of them like a man possessed.

Beneath him Zoe writhed, a sting of nonsense words and curses falling from her lips as she begged and pleaded and praised them both.

Luca's face was a rictus of pleasure and seeing him, staring into his handsome face, had Ryan throbbing in all kinds of unexpected ways until he couldn't keep his climax at bay anymore.

He reached around, almost blindly, to detach one of the nipple clamps and, without direction, Luca followed his lead with the other. They released at the same time and Zoe erupted between them, bucking and arching as she screamed her completion.

The tightening of her hot channel squeezing his length was too much and he bellowed as he gave over to the sheer bliss that coursed through his veins. His thrusts were irregular and erratic and so were Luca's as he too shouted out his pleasure. The three of them perfectly synced.

For long minutes they all collapsed onto the bed, panting and sucking in great draughts of air as their clammy bodies cooled. Then Ryan managed to find enough energy to see to himself and fetch a damp cloth to clean Zoe up before they all fell back into an exhausted sleep.

* * *

I t was a couple of hours later that Zoe was woken, sated and content, by a faint, rustling sound.

She opened her eyes to find Luca searching around for his clothes.

"Please don't go..." she implored then drifted off as it occurred to her that maybe he'd had his fill and was done.

He turned to look at her, then flicked a look to Ryan who was snoring lightly. "I thought you'd want some privacy," he told her honestly.

She shook her head. "No, if you leave it'll just make me feel like a cheap whore." She patted the mattress next to her. "Come back to bed. Stay with us."

Her eyes drifted closed, and she sighed in satisfaction when he did just that.

Chapter Seven

They spent the next seven days sleeping late after their nights of fun and debauchery. Checking out all the many activities in the afternoons. Dining together in different restaurants around the resort in the evenings. Before going back to their secluded cabana to do it all again.

On the eighth day everything came to an end.

Zoe tried to get her head around exactly how she was feeling as she packed the last of her luggage before they caught the complimentary shuttle to the airport. Luca was leaving today, too.

It was a holiday romance, she told herself. Nothing more.

But it had been so full on that the thought of going back felt empty somehow.

She tried to shake herself out of it. What the heck would Ryan think if he thought she was pining over another man after he'd been generous enough to give her this. Besides, that's not how it was. Not quite, anyway. She didn't want Luca... well, no more than she wanted her husband.

It was just the usual let down after that exciting holiday high, she told herself stoically.

Post-holiday blues, that's what it was, Zoe told herself a month later when she caught herself feeling down after getting back to the drudgery of day-to-day life. That and the miserable British weather plus a dose of empty nest syndrome now the twins were gone.

Ryan was feeling it too. He was quiet and a little melancholy.

Except all too often her thoughts drifted back to those steamy nights with both Luca and Ryan and how alive and excited and cherished they'd made her feel.

There were so many things they didn't get to explore. Ryan had admitted to being bi-curious since they returned home, but that hadn't been a huge part of their holiday dynamic and now Zoe wished it had. She wished Ryan had had the chance for more.

They'd exchanged phone numbers and in a moment of weakness Zoe had massaged Luca, giving him their address and inviting him to come and stay. She'd done it for Ryan as much as herself, hoping it would cheer him up.

Luca hadn't replied.

Maybe it was better that way.

Besides, she knew he had a busy job in Italy, and they lived in the UK. It might not be a million miles away, but it was enough. And if he had come, they'd both have to go through this all over again when it was time for him to leave.

* * *

It was almost eight weeks to the day when there was a knock on their door. Zoe was in the middle of cooking Sunday roast dinner.

"Are you expecting anyone?" Zoe called to Ryan, who sat distractedly watching the TV in the lounge.

"No," he replied, but didn't make any move to get the door.

Zoe sighed and dried her hands on a tea towel before hurrying to answer it.

At first, she just stared at the hot guy with his tanned complexion, slightly curling hair and sharp, expensive suit. Then she looked into his melted chocolate eyes and squealed before launching herself at him.

Luca laughed as he caught her swinging her around and kissing her soundly. When he finally put her down, Ryan was there, seeing what all the commotion was about.

"Zoe, what...?"

The two men went quiet and looked at each other for long seconds. Then they both seemed to move at once. Ryan gripped Luca by the shoulder and Luca curled his hand around Ryan's neck and their mouths clashed in a kiss every bit as passionate as the one he and Zoe had just shared.

She was stunned at how much that turned her on.

When they pulled apart, Zoe squeezed herself in between them and for a moment they all just hugged before everyone started talking at once.

"What are you doing here?"

"Is the offer to stay still open?"

How long can you stop?"

They laughed and subsided and Ryan ushered them all into the living room.

"I missed you guys," Luca said quietly.

"We missed you, too," Ryan told him, cutting a glance her way. "Both of us."

Zoe just nodded as tears prickled her eyes. Could she do this again? Could she have the dream a second time and remain in one piece when Luca left again?

The silence stretched for a while and Ryan hugged her

close. He knew, she realised. He knew exactly what she was feeling because he was feeling it himself.

Luca sucked in a breath and his cheeks puffed up when he blew it out. His eyes were glued to his feet. "All my adult life I feel like I've been looking for what you two share," he suddenly revealed. "Male, female; I wasn't fussy. I guess you realised that about me by now," he said with a wry chuckle. He looked at them both then. "And when I found it, it wasn't with one person, but two. Two people who already had each other but allowed me in for a short time and let me experience something more."

Zoe felt the tension in Ryan and squeezed his hand, but they kept silent and waited for Luca to finish.

"I thought it would be okay," he revealed. "I thought I could go home and just think of it as a perfect slice of time... but I couldn't. I couldn't get you out of my mind. Either of you. I wanted more. So, when Zoe contacted me, I decided to see if I could move my work to the UK."

Zoe sucked in a breath. Was he saying what she thought he was saying? She hardly dared to hope.

"And did you?" Ryan asked warily. She looked at her husband. He didn't want to get his hopes up either, she realised, but she could feel the excitement in the speed of his pulse. He was just as invested as she was.

"I did," Luca confirmed. He speared them both with an intense gaze. "So, the question is should I just get on the next plane back to Italy? Or do the pair of you want to see where this thing leads us?"

She thought Luca was holding his breath. His jaw was clenched, and his hands fisted as he waited for an answer.

Zoe looked at Ryan. This wasn't a decision she could make alone even though she already knew what she wanted.

She wanted to watch them together. She wanted to see

Luca gagging on Ryan's cock. She wanted Luca to fuck her while Ryan fucked him.

There were so many dark and dirty fantasies she wanted to explore. But more than anything, she wanted them all to be together. The three of them.

She wanted this to be the start of a beautiful reality.

She wanted this to be more.

Moore and Moreno.

Even their names matched; pointed in the direction she wanted this to go.

Ryan looked back at her and they spoke with their eyes. Then a huge smile bloomed over Zoe's face and was reflected in her husband's.

They turned back to look at Luca.

"Hell, yes!" they both said at once.

Kayla & Marcus Thorne

Kayla Mountbatten breezed into her brother's study at the stately home they shared in the leafy Windsor countryside.

"Do you fancy a trip to the States," she asked the tow-headed man who sat behind the desk. "I'm feeling the need to let loose. It's been too long."

Marcus grinned and threw down his pen. "I wondered how long it would be before you asked, after Royal Ascot, Wimbledon, and the Henley Regatta all back-to-back and all that dressing up in feathery hats and schmoozing you had to do."

"Ugh!" Kayla snorted in a definitely *un*ladylike manner. "Don't remind me."

She liked to dress up, but her selection of corsets and thigh-high boots were a far cry from what was considered haute couture by the ladies of the British social season calendar.

She was independently wealthy, but they had agreed, soon after their father's death, that she would help Marcus maintain and run the estate and its associated businesses.

He was the heir, of course, the reigning Duke, since their father had passed.

Kayla was a mere 'Lady'. And she would have preferred to be nothing at all.

Her lifestyle - *their* lifestyle - didn't sync well with being so closely related to the royal family. They both would have preferred anonymity, but until they each found a life partner - if that ever happened - they had each other's backs.

They had to. It was the only way they could ensure their kinky secrets were kept safe from the public eye and didn't cause the type of scandal the family would never recover from.

It was a good job the Queen no longer locked people up in the Tower of London and executed them, because that was undoubtedly what would have happened, in days of old, if word ever got out.

Of course, she and Marcus would probably have had rather a good time with all those torture devices.

But not on the receiving end, though.

One thing she was not, was some meek submissive. She wasn't called Lady Thorne for nothing.

The name alone appealed to her perverted sense of humour. And Thorne was the name they'd both adopted to keep their identities concealed, along with traveling to overseas kink clubs, where they were far more anonymous. No point in soiling your own doorstep, as it were.

"Well, you're in luck," Marcus pulled her out of her reverie. "I'm pretty sure I can free up some time in a couple of days, so you can get your fix in."

Kayla narrowed her eyes and scoffed at him. "Like you don't need to get your freak on as well, *milord*," she teased.

* * *

Marcus looked around the Detroit Club and just stopped for a moment, closed his eyes to absorb the atmosphere. Regardless of where the club was, or what its reputation, they all had a similar kind of ambience. The sounds and smells of sex and leather. The distinctive cacophony of squeals and moans; of impact strikes and writhing bodies.

This particular club wasn't his favourite place. It was a bit seedy and slightly squalid, but Kayla favoured it. In her mind, it was the last place anyone would ever expect to find members of the British aristocracy, so there was less chance of them being recognised, and he guessed she was right about that.

Their practices were okay. If they hadn't been, he would have overruled his sister, no matter what. But they always made a point of looking out for each other, regardless.

Not quite going as far as DM'ing for each other. That would just be weird. He did not want to watch his sister having sex, and the same applied vice versa. But they never scened at the same time, just in case something went down that they didn't want to get involved in.

They couldn't afford any scandal in their lives and for the past ten years, it had all worked out fine. Though since their father had died a couple of years ago, it had been a little more pressured, with his newly acquired Dukedom and the 'Eligible Batchelor' status that went with it. The damn press was all over him like a rash these days, so they needed to take extra care.

Ironically, Kayla was the one who was more anal about it, even though he had much more to lose. Some of the business dealings he'd inherited, which relied solely on his name and status, certainly wouldn't weather that kind of disgrace. They really needed to diversify.

"Oh, my fucking god!" Kayla swore inelegantly beside him. No one who heard her potty mouth would ever imagine she was a bona fide 'lady' of the realm.

"What is it?" he asked, shaking himself out of his reverie and walking over to where she had her hands on her hips and was staring at a board full of fairly tacky looking prints.

"Bloody hell!" he exclaimed when he realised what she was looking at.

Marcus reached over her shoulder and ripped down the offensive picture. "Where the hell did they get this?" he asked, studying the photograph of his sister, dressed in a red, waist cinching corset which emphasised her ample breasts and hips, and a pair of her trademark thigh-high boots. She was brandishing a whip and her long hair hung in a rather dishevelled cloud around her shoulders.

It was exactly the kind of shot the paparazzi would have a damn field day with.

It was printed on cheap paper and Marcus ripped into two and then in two again, before crumpling it up. "What the hell are you doing now?" he demanded of his sister, as she continued to mess about with the other pictures on the long wall board.

"I'm moving them around a bit so there's not a gap," she muttered, using her long, painted fingernails to claw out the pins that held the cheap display together. "I don't want someone replacing the damn thing."

Okay, that was probably sensible.

"Are you sure you want to stick around?" he asked, looking at the 'hall of fame' display to ensure there weren't any other nasty surprises. "This sort of thing is unprofessional and extremely invasive of people's privacy."

"Well, we're here now, so we might as well stay," Kayla replied with a sigh. "And honestly, I'm glad we found that and did the necessary damage control."

It was a small mercy, but she was right. Still, Marcus couldn't help the feeling of foreboding that settled around him. He'd be extra vigilant this evening, and he'd give her tonight, but after this, he was going to insist on somewhere a bit more up market, regardless.

He wasn't putting them at risk like this again.

* * *

Kayla felt the stress seep out of her bones like it was a physical thing, the minute she stepped inside the private playroom. God, she needed this.

It was with an encompassing pleasure that she surreptitiously watched the muscled male who already kneeled, his gaze dutifully downcast while he waited for her.

Despite her satisfaction, she deliberately ignored him and instead closed the blackout blind to make the scene private.

After that, she busied herself laying out the toys she wanted, making him wait a while longer before she stepped up before him.

He was well trained, this one. Too good for this place, really.

She'd contacted him before she made the trip to see if he was free to meet her here... he was one of her favourite playthings, and she happily paid his expenses for that luxury.

With his hands still clasped behind his back, he leaned forward and kissed her boots. She watched his ripped abdominal muscles condense and contract as he moved. It was fair to say she had a type and Darius ticked all the boxes.

Tall, handsome, tanned, buff and a masochist.

He wasn't necessarily a true submissive, but his desire for pain as an aphrodisiac married well with her own sadistic steak. She didn't need a man to be completely servile. In fact, she expected he was one of her favourites, precisely because he wasn't.

She needed someone who had a strong enough character to take her on and give her what she needed after the pain and been dispensed, but she had never wanted to be responsible for having to give a partner his every direction.

She just wanted one who would take the kind of pain she liked to dish out.

She was open gender on that, although generally a man could take more of the particular torment she liked to administer, but she scened with women as well, when she was in the mood.

When it came to sex, however, she was all for cock and Darius here had the perfect specimen.

After a couple of years of scening together, he knew her well; he knew what to expect and knew what she liked. They never had any contact outside arranging scenes, but it worked for both of them.

She wondered, briefly, if he'd be open to some private play. The incident earlier on with the picture had shaken her. But, regretfully, that would probably leave her true identity open to risk.

She shelved the idea with a sigh.

"Up," she ordered, and he sat back on his haunches immediately.

Kayla walked around him, her fingers tangling in his thick, black hair. "I'm feeling ruthless this evening," she warned him. "I want to whip you and see your skin welt under my lashes. Is that something you can get on board with tonight?"

"Yes, ma'am,' he replied, his rich, deep voice reaching the few dormant parts left inside of her.

She eyed his strong shoulders and the unblemished skin of his back, imagining how it would look after she'd lashed him. The mere thought had heat blooming between her thighs, and her nipples peaking and chaffing inside her boned corset. Her fingers tingled with the need to put her mark on him, but she sucked in a breath and calmed the urgency. It would be better for them both if she took this slowly and allowed the moment to build.

"What about sex?" she asked. "Is that on the table tonight?" He'd never denied her, but she wasn't going to assume. Negotiation and consent were the bedrock of this lifestyle. They meant everything. Plus, the one drawback of being in the US was that sex was generally illegal in clubs. Places like this though, they generally looked the other way as long as you greased the right palms and used a private room.

"For you, always, my lady," he agreed, and any last tension she'd been harbouring slipped away. A good workout with her whip hand, the sadistic high of torment and control, and a bout of rough sex with a couple of orgasms, and she'd be set for another few weeks.

"Strip," she ordered, and moved to a chair close by so she could watch him remove his faded black jeans, which was the only thing he wore.

She crooked her finger at him when he was done and beckoned him towards her. "How much pain are you looking for tonight, Darius?" she asked, dragging the pointed tip of her stiletto heel along his thigh, hard enough to leave a mark, when he finally stood in front of her.

"As much as you want to dish out, Lady Thorne," he replied, his blue eyes blazing as he looked at her.

God, she loved that face, that body. Gorgeous didn't come much better than him.

That he matched her kinks so well was the very decadent icing on a damn fine cake. One she fully intended to take her fill of.

She tapped her lip with one long, manicured finger as she appraised him. Like she was thinking about it.

It was all part of the game. She knew exactly how she was going to play things.

"I think I'd like you strapped to the St Andrews Cross today," she told him and relished the delicious shiver that rolled through his very fine frame.

He was as excited about this as she was.

She used the quick release, velcro fastenings to cuff his wrists and ankles. With Darius, the restraints were really just for show. It was part of the power trip for both of them. He would have remained just as still if she'd simply ordered him to hold on to the loops. But she appreciated the easy removal. She hated having to faff around with buckles when she was ready to take things to the next level. It seriously killed her vibe.

She rubbed her hands up and down his muscled back, appreciating his form. She'd appreciate it even more when it was patterned by her leather.

Digging her long nails into his fine rump and giving it a vicious squeeze, she left him to find her favourite six-foot-long bullwhip. It had been made especially for her and had a particularly satisfying cracker, although it would be wrong to say that its bark was worse that its bite. They were both equally ferocious.

Shaking it out, along with her wrists, she then rolled her shoulders and neck to loosen up before throwing the first lash without any warning.

Darius threw his head back at the strike, but made no sound, just sucked in a breath as he savoured the burn.

She didn't need him to be vocal. In fact, she preferred it when her men were quiet. She liked to see them absorb the pain and revel in it; internalise it and make it their own. That did far more for her than hearing a strong man scream like a girl. Although she could appreciate the odd grating growl.

She landed another and another, congratulating herself on the even welts that rose up across his shoulders and down his back.

Judiciously, she avoided his tailbone and his kidneys before flicking the single tail to slash across his very fine ass.

Picking up the pace, she crisscrossed the lines to form a diamond pattern on his skin. The biting sound of the whip's popper filled the room with its song and Kayla lost herself in the rhythm.

The melody filled her soul, and she submerged herself in it, hitting top space with remarkable ease. She only got this with Darius. The perfection of their harmony always blew her away.

Throwing down the whip, she closed in behind him, running her hands all over the raised welts that now decorated his skin. She revelled in the quiet hiss he let out between his teeth as she reignited the pain, then reached around until she could palm his heavy, straining cock.

"I want you, now. Free yourself," she murmured in his ear, squeezing his blessed manhood hard before crouching down to detach the ankle cuffs, while he took care of his wrists and then grabbed a condom.

Like a finely choreographed dance which had been practised many times, Darius spun around and pushed Kayla onto the bed. Her skirt rode up and underneath it, she was naked. He fell on top of her, and shoved his cock into her wet, waiting heat, setting a punishing tempo right from the outset.

He palmed the generous mounds of her breasts and feasted on the nipples he freed from their satin cups, and she arched into his mouth.

Kayla fisted both of her hands in to his hair, pulling tight and spurring him on, almost smothering him with her ample bosom. She wound her legs around his thighs and dug the heels of her shoes into his flesh until he bucked against her even harder, bottoming out against her cervix again and again, relentlessly.

Her fingers strayed to the welts on his shoulders, playing the raised lines like they were a piano. At the same time, she found that gloriously fleshy place where his neck met his shoulder and bit down hard, inciting his pounding impetus, knowing she would leave the very personal mark of her teeth on him for the next few days. The thought alone had heat sizzling through her veins.

Her abdomen tensed and the coil of her climax squeezed and contracted as he fucked her seven ways to Sunday. Until finally, like a spring that had been wound too tight and burst apart, the orgasm broke over her.

She screamed her pleasure and sank her nails into Darius' shoulders, knowing they'd break the skin.

His breath, his rhythm, faltered, became choppy, and she dragged her fingers down his back, giving him a final bite of pain to latch onto for his own fulfilment.

He threw back his head and the cords in his neck stood out in stark relief as he poured out his pleasure before they both surfed on the wave of completion until it dispersed.

Their breathing was ragged, and she could see the pulse pounding in his neck. He scattered rough kisses across her collarbone and regained a little of his composure before lifting his head and spearing her with his intense blue eyes. "One day, I'll get you out of these clothes, my lady," he panted. "And we'll do this naked."

Kayla smiled and shook her head. "No way," she replied. She was comfortable in her form fitted corsets, and confident in her role, but she preferred not to put her rolls of fat on show, especially with the foil of Darius's perfection as a backdrop.

"Is that a challenge, Lady Thorne?" he asked, his eyes never leaving hers.

Yeah, definitely not submissive. But then, neither was she.

"That's a fact, my darling," she purred, pushing him away and moving to clean herself up while he disposed of the condom.

"We'll see," he chuckled as he dressed, covering all the lovely marks she'd decorated him with in a black silk shirt. It was almost enough to make her pout.

"What?" she asked, frowning when his words registered.

Darius strode over until he was standing toe to toe with

her, and she had to tip her head back to look at him, despite her high heels.

"I'm getting out of here," he told her, instead of repeating himself. "There's an odd vibe about this place tonight, which I don't like. You should get out of here too."

Kayla nodded her head absently, still slightly bemused by his previous words. "I will, as soon as Marcus is ready."

Darius nodded once, then shocked her completely by grabbing a fistful of her hair and taking her mouth in a hot, hard kiss.

Well... that was a first.

"And we will definitely be getting naked at some point, Lady Thorne," he told her in no uncertain terms before he turned on his heel and strode out of the door, leaving her touching her fingers to her swollen lips and wondering what the hell had just happened.

* * *

While Kayla was in her scene, Marcus put the word out that he was looking for a submissive who was up for some impact play with oral and toys; hold the sex. He wouldn't take that chance in this kind of venue, which conveniently turned a blind eye, even if he was suited up. Maybe he should have done the same as his sister, and had someone meet him here, but sadist or not, he drew the line at encouraging a lone woman to walk the streets of Detroit if she wasn't familiar with them.

He'd turned away a couple of women already on one pretext or another, but the feeling had been mutual. They just wanted to get their rocks off, like immediately, and weren't prepared to wait.

They'd looked far too jaded and maybe slightly high and couldn't understand his need to have his sisters back, and that just grated on him. Besides, he never mixed BDSM with any kind of opiate, not even alcohol, so he was never going to be going there, so their impatience worked in his favour.

The third girl to come his way looked like an angel. And she looked far too good to be in this dive. Marcus was shocked at his immediate, overwhelming desire to shelter her from all the bad things in life.

Which made no sense at all. She was a stranger; he didn't know her story or her background and likely the wide-eyed innocence that poured off of her was just an illusion. She was here in a skanky club in the bowels of seedy Detroit, after all. But he still couldn't shake the feeling.

Unlike the others, she stayed happy to bide her time and wait while Kayla finished her scene. She seemed almost awed that he wanted to protect his sister, and she gazed at him with big blue eyes that looked at him like he'd hung the moon.

That made him a bit uncomfortable. He was about to do dirty, nasty things to her. But the concept that no one had ever done anything nice for this angelic looking girl had him wanting to take care of her all over again. So much so that he made a determined effort to keep the conversation as light and nondescript as possible. The weather, sports... that was a bit of a non-starter. She didn't know much about tennis, golf or horses and he didn't know much about baseball.

Books: that occupied them for a while. She surprised him with her knowledge there. With her spun gold hair and eyes like saucers of tropical blue, she didn't look like the type to read the kinds of bloody thrillers he enjoyed. Her innate intelligence shined through too, and once again he was wondering what she was doing in a dive like this one.

Nope, not going there. And who was he to judge, anyway. He was here.

They'd just finished discussing safe words and agreeing on the traffic light system, when Kayla's boy toy came striding out of the private room they were using. Marcus gave him a polite nod, which was returned in the same manner. He didn't know the guy but recognised him from the number of times his sister hooked up with him.

Marcus knew instinctively that he was someone else who was out of place here, too. God, they needed to do better. Kayla was just going to have to suck it up.

He took his sister aside and spoke to her in low tones. "Keep your eyes open and you head down," he told her. "There's an atmosphere in this place I don't like this evening."

He scanned the large warehouse space. They were on an upper level, tucked away in the corner where there was little traffic. He'd booked this particular room for precisely that reason. But something still wasn't sitting right with him.

Kayla nodded her agreement, her brow furrowing as she followed his gaze around the ground floor area. Everything seemed to be carrying on as normal. Nothing really looked out of place, so he wasn't sure why he felt so on edge. It was just a gut feeling.

Hell, maybe it was just the general level of duplicity he and Kayla lived under because of this lifestyle and the conflict with their social standing. Perhaps he was getting too old for all this subterfuge.

In their twenties, they'd embraced all the cloak and dagger intrigue like it was just some kind of lark, but lately - maybe since he'd inherited his father's title and holdings - it was all getting to be too much.

He sighed and shelved his misgivings. No one was going to recognise them here. They were about as far away from the British aristocracy as they could possibly get. He was letting his mind run away with him.

Perhaps he was more stressed than he thought.

He smiled at the patiently waiting submissive. Marcus hadn't even asked her name. He was going to change that, he decided, as he ushered her into the playroom.

Damn, she was beautiful, he thought, as he followed her inside. She was wearing a kind of floaty chemise type garment in a silvery colour that just added to the whole angelic aura, and a flat pair of sandals that wound up her calves with ribbons.

Normally he would have made her strip off until there was nothing but bare skin, but he'd changed his mind as well as his initial thoughts on the kind of scene he was going to play out, since seeing her. He was going to keep her dressed; the devil inside him would enjoy defiling her illusion of innocence. The whole scenario appealed to his wicked mind.

"You may call me Mar... Master Thorne," he informed her, wondering at the slip he'd almost made. This girl undid him. "What's your name?" he asked as he sat down on the bed and tried not to think about whether his sister had just used it.

He beckoned her to stand between his open thighs. She moved dutifully, but took so long to answer that he wasn't certain she was going to. Still, he was surprised a club name hadn't tripped off of her tongue. Maybe she was as new to this as she looked.

"It's okay," he soothed, as he ran his hands up her silky legs. "You don't have to tell me."

Marcus's hands roamed under the short, flippy skirt of her dress until he could palm her ass. She was wearing a minute excuse for a thong, which pleased him, and he kneaded her bare ass cheeks in readiness for the hand spanking he was planning to give her.

She looked at him guilelessly and Marcus had to bite his tongue to stop himself from demanding to know what she was doing in a place like this. It wasn't his business, and he wasn't normally that kind of double standards arsehole.

Instead, he tugged on her wrist and pulled her over his knee. The breath was forced out of her with a small grunt, as she landed heavily, not expecting the move or the ferocity of it. It made his cock harden even more than the anticipation of all the things he wanted to do to her.

He wanted to manhandle her; he wanted to despoil that pure, wholesome image. To have her gasping and screaming while he spanked her and forced pleasure onto her. Then hear her crying and gagging as he ruthlessly fucked her face.

After all that, he could sit her on his knee and soothe her; stroke her golden hair, dishevelled by his hands, while her hot, reddened backside burned through the fabric of his trousers.

And that was exactly what he planned to do, he thought, with devilish glee.

He rubbed each globe of her perfect ass. Maybe when he was done spanking her, he'd leave a bite mark on that perfect skin for her to remember him by. He bit back a groan and landed the first slap instead.

She gasped, and her skin bloomed with his handprint. He enjoyed the sight so much that he stopped and looked his fill, before matching the other side.

The little noises she made were addictive, and soon he was peppering her ass, up and down, side to side. Every single inch, until there wasn't a millimetre that wasn't reddened by his hand, just so he could hear more of them.

But he wanted more than that. He wanted her sobbing; he wanted her tears and then he wanted to stick his hard, aching cock down her throat.

But first things first. First, she needed to be punished like the naughty little temptress that she was, and Marcus went to work on the backs of her thighs and her sit spots. She kicked her legs, so he pinned then between his own. She wrapped both her arms around his other leg, and he could see her shoulders jerking with the sobs that she was trying so hard to keep silent.

Not good enough. He wanted those too, and he planned to keep spanking her until she gave them to him. Or used her safe word. But because he was feeling generous, he decided to tell her so, at least.

"I want your tears, pet. I want to hear you cry. Give that to me."

She didn't. Not immediately, anyway. Her shoulders quaked a little harder, then there was a sniffle and a hiccup before she finally gave it up. It pleased him, probably more than it should have. He had a feeling she was naturally quiet and never made very much noise. That she submitted to the demand for him, was a huge aphrodisiac.

When she was limp and sobbing, albeit quietly, still, over his knee, he finally stopped and stroked his hand across her heated flesh.

He took a moment to soothe her and waited for the

quaking of her shoulder to subside before pushing her down onto her knees.

The sight of her at his feet, the tracks of her tears glistening in silvery trails down her porcelain cheeks, had him harder than rock and he struggled to unbutton his fly. Her hands fluttered, and he knew she wanted to help him, but she fisted them to stop herself and settled them at her sides like the well-trained sub she was.

"Open," he grunted, when his straining shaft was finally free. The words were barely out of his mouth, before she was ready, her little pink tongue poking out slightly to accept his offering.

He made her wait again, just for the hell of it, painting her lips with his pre-cum. Then, when she would have flicked her tongue across his slit, he grasped a fistful of her golden curls and shoved into her waiting mouth with one brutal thrust.

She choked and her eyes streamed before she regained her equilibrium and swallowed around his thick length. The sight of her pretty rosebud mouth stretched wide around him made him savage and he set up a merciless pace, his fists in her hair pulling her onto him at the same time as he pushed, so she had zero control. The urge to defile her like this was fierce and untamed. It lacked his usual finesse, but Marcus didn't care. She brought out something primitive and feral within him. Something that had been buried under years of duty and the heavy veneer of keeping up appearances.

The freedom she granted him was indescribable. Like he could finally be himself, even though it had never occurred to him that he wasn't true to his own desires.

He felt the surge of his climax galloping down his spine and pooling in his scrotum.

He couldn't last.

He gritted his teeth as he fought to keep back the tide, to

enjoy her like this for just a few moments more, but it was almost impossible.

And then her hand fluttered between his legs, whispering ever so lightly over his balls, tightening them further, before she found his perineum and pressed down on it. He didn't even have time to warn her, although he was pretty sure she knew the consequences of her actions before his seed surged forth with unstoppable velocity and hit the back of her throat. She redoubled her efforts, swallowing around him as he threw his head back and roared his completion.

Then he lowered his head to look at her, once he'd grasped some semblance of control and her limpid blue eyes, wet from him gagging on his cock, were waiting to envelop him and he drowned in the depths of those cerulean pools while his heart stuttered.

This vixen, with the appearance of an angel, had cast some kind of spell on him and he was ruined.

Marcus collapsed on the bed and scooped her up in his arms, holding her close and burying his face in the perfumed fall of her silky hair while he regained his wrecked equilibrium. He cradled her gently, something he found he liked far more than was good for him, before he surged to his feet and turned around, laying her out on the bed.

It was time for her to have her reward.

She hissed a little when her butt hit the sheets and Marcus leaned over to rearrange her clothing, still enjoying the angelic illusion. Her outfit was secured at the shoulder with thin straps which were tied into bows. He undid just one of them to reveal a single breast, then bent his head to take it in his mouth and lave it with affection. She arched into him, but instead of giving her more, he pulled back, banking his satisfaction at her little mewl of disappointment, while he lifted the hem of her skirt.

She had wrecked him and now he was going to wreck her.

Digging around in his toy bag he'd brought with him, he found the butterfly vibrator he was searching for and strapped it around her slim thighs, switching the dial on low.

She wriggled a little, but just to get comfortable.

Marcus hid his wicked grin. That would soon change.

He retrieved a decent sized butt plug, removed it from the packaging so she was reassured it was new, and lubed it up right in front of her. Her eyes widened when he put it down on the side table next to her, right in her line of sight, so she could get a good look at the ribs and nodules covering the surface. But she made no move to stop him as he shackled both her ankles in one hand and proceeded to ease first one finger, then another past the tight ring of muscle of her sphincter.

She gave an almost silent whimper, and he watched the muscle jump in her abdomen as he started to scissor his fingers to prepare her for the plug.

She sucked in a breath and grimaced, but she was still unnaturally quiet. Dragging his fingers in and out past the plethora of nerves in her anus, turned those breaths to shallow pants.

He withdrew his fingers, and she relaxed for a moment before he reached for the plug and her wide eyes tracked his movements all the way back to her rosy, red, upturned butt. He placed the tip on her pucker and teased her with it for a while, until she didn't know what to expect. Then he pressed it inside in one long, slow, inexorable glide, his eyes flicking between her face and the silicon phallus as the multiple ridges, each a little wider than the last, disappeared inside her stretching rectum.

She was panting in full when the toy was finally fully inserted, and her pucker shrank to clutch around the narrowed base. But he still had one more surprise for her, and he chuckled when her mouth formed a little O when he switched on the remote which had it stirring, gently - for now - inside her.

Marcus lowered her legs and positioned her feet so they were splayed wide, her knees bent and drawn up, so she was fully open to his ministrations. He attached a spreader bar to prevent her from closing her legs and used the second set of cuffs attached to the device to shackle her wrists so she could neither lower her knees nor lift her arms.

He left her in that position, both toys quietly vibrating while he went to wash his hands. Then, while his back was turned, and she was least expecting it, he dialled the vibration on both remotes up to high and when her surprised gasp filled the air, he added the surprise punch that was packed into the butt plug he'd used. A literal one which caused the toy to stretch and contract inside her, like she was being fucked.

She lasted mere seconds. By the time he'd dried his hands and swung around to face her, she was already shaking with her climax.

He intended that to be the first of many.

Walking back to the bed, he dialled down the intensity and his gaze was drawn to her heaving chest. He perched next to her and took a long leisurely swipe at her nipple with the broad of his tongue, while his fingers unerringly found her core. She was wet and labia just a little puffy. He drew his fingers up and down, but she was getting used to his tactics of lulling her and then firing with both barrels. It was time to change things up and keep her guessing, so instead of plunging his fingers inside her waiting channel, he stroked her gently while he suckled at her breast. The next climax, when it came, rolled over her softly, and she arched into his touch.

He didn't give her any respite this time though, the second her wetness covered his fingers, he was forcing her upwards again and again, finding that sensitive, textured place inside her honeyed depths and crooking his fingers until he wrung the pleasure out of her. He notched up the dual vibrators and nibbled and pinched at her nipples, then pressed the butterfly down harder on her sensitive flesh and rotated it over her clit until she broke again.

Her breathing was laboured now and her climaxes noisy. Gone was the composed and hushed submissive who had entered, and in her place was a wild thing who bucked and strained and begged him.

"Oh god, no! No more, please," she sobbed, shaking her head wildly as he forced her up once more.

"I c-can't, I really can't. No!" She screamed and writhed, trying in vain to evade his touch, but Marcus was ruthless, and her safe word was nowhere to be heard.

Finally, when her chest was heaving with her laboured breath and real tears streamed down her face, he relented. Her body still jolted reflexively as he uncuffed her from the spreader bar and helped her stretch out her shaking legs. He massaged her thighs and calves with strong fingers to help get her blood flow back, then did the same for her arms and shoulders.

She whimpered in relief this time, and he leaned down and stole the sweet sounds gently from her lips. Normally kissing the sub he played with, whether it was a stranger or a regular hook up, was a no-no for him, but this time Marcus couldn't help himself.

When her breathing eventually slowed and he'd massaged all her muscles, he settled himself properly on the bed, pulled her into his arms and cuddled her on his knee.

He might have stayed like that indefinitely, if Kayla hadn't started hammering on the door and then come barging in to disturb them.

* * *

Kayla checked her watch. She'd expected Marcus to be finished by now, but clearly the little sub he'd found had tickled his fancy.

She frowned and looked around, realising that she hadn't seen a dungeon monitor all night, which was unusual, even for a place like this. Peering over the industrial railing to the main floor below, her frown deepened. Was she imagining it, or were there fewer people around suddenly? These places usually got slammed later at night on the weekends. A frisson of unease raced through her, and she almost didn't look at her phone when the message chime sounded.

Her breath stuck in her throat when she read the text from Darius.

Get out of there. NOW! The club's being raided.

She almost dropped it as she fumbled to grab her bag and get word to Marcus.

God, this could be disastrous. The last thing they needed was to be arrested and carted off for identification. The consequences didn't bear thinking about.

She hammered on the door of the playroom Marcus was using and prayed he wasn't *in flagrante delicto* when she lost patience and threw open the door.

"We need to get out of here," she whisper shouted, her voice quivering in a way that she truly hated. "The club's being raided. Hurry!"

The sub Marcus was with gave a little yelp and dived off the bed, almost collapsing when her legs gave way, and she'd have landed in a heap on the floor if Marcus hadn't grasped her by the arm to keep her upright.

He snagged his bag, stuff toppled out, but a quick glance proved it was nothing of importance, like his phone or the car keys. The two of them always kept everything on their person. Never trusting their belongings not to fall into the wrong hands, and right now that was a godsend.

As they piled out of the room, there was a commotion below. Kayla risked a quick peek then reared back as she spotted countless police officers followed by a news team with a damn camera hot on their heels.

"Oh my god, this is the stuff of nightmares," she muttered. "What are we going to do?"

She turned to Marcus for direction. "We can't get out downstair, is there an exit up here? A fire-escape or something?"

"Shit," Marcus cursed under his breath and looked around, searching for something that might help them. "Even if there is, I'd be surprised if they don't have it covered."

He spoke the words that she'd been thinking. Nobody mounted a raid without having all the exits surrounded.

"I might know a way," the timid voice of the blonde sub, scratchy from all the screaming she'd been doing - yeah, Kayla hadn't been able to block that out - cut into her whirling thoughts.

"What is it?" Marcus demanded.

"Everyone stay where you are and don't move," came the order from the floor below through some kind of megaphone. They were out of time.

The pounding of heavy boots could be heard at the far end of the walkway, just out of sight, as someone - several someone's - ran up the metal staircase.

"This way," the girl whispered hoarsely, pulling at Marcus's arm. There was a door which Kayla had assumed led to another playroom, but right now, she'd settle for hiding, if she thought they had a chance of waiting this out.

They all piled through as quickly and quietly as possible

and found themselves in a stairwell. Marcus had the presence of mind to pause for a moment and heave the long metal bar into place. It might buy them some time, if nothing else. Provided they didn't meet someone coming from down below.

"Where does this lead?" Marcus asked, doubt and urgency fighting for supremacy in his voice.

"To the fire exit," the girl told him. "But I have an idea... there's another way."

They followed her because they had no choice. Behind them led certain arrest and neither of them was familiar enough with this place to know of anything better. At least this way there might be a chance. Slim though it was.

Above them, someone was rattling the door and shouting. *"There's no escape. All the exits are sealed. It's better if you come quietly."*

The girl whimpered and, for a moment, she faltered.

"Keep going," Marcus hissed. "They couldn't have seen us, so they're just covering themselves."

The two of them dashed down the steps in front of her and Kayla did her best to keep up, but as much as she loved her sky-high heels, they weren't made for running, and much less downstairs. She'd be lucky if she didn't break her neck.

When she caught up, Marcus was helping the girl haul some kind of steel roller hatch open to reveal... well, she wasn't sure what was behind it.

"It's the old stock chute," she told them, as if she'd read Kayla's mind. "Left over from when this was a warehouse, so people didn't have to haul everything up and down the stairs."

Marcus stuck his head inside and gave the metal structure a hard shove. "It looks stable enough," he declared.

Right now, Kayla wasn't sure that was even a consideration, considering the alternatives.

"Where does it lead to?" she asked. "And how do we know there won't be someone waiting for us at the end?" That was the only thing she was interested in right now.

"It dumps into a kind of storage cellar," she told them. "It hasn't been used for years and has one of those old-fashioned trapdoor things to get out of, which is probably overgrown since it borders the woods." She peered into the void of blackness. "It's probably not very clean and I'm not sure how easy it will be to get out, but we might manage to lie low until everyone's left, at least."

On the floor they'd just fled, a monotonous battering made them aware that the door was clearly being booted in. They didn't have much time.

"Get down there," Marcus whispered to the sub. "Kayla, you follow."

The girl swung her bare legs onto the chute, but that's where things went wrong. Her bare skin stuck to the metal so she couldn't easily slide. She whimpered and wriggled to try and move herself and above them there was the sound of splintering as the heavy door started to give.

"Marcus, take her down on your knee," Kayla directed. "We need to get moving."

Marcus looked from her to the girl to the noise a short half-floor above. "Will you be able to close the shutter?" he asked.

"I'll manage," she muttered. She'd just swing her not inconsiderable weight on it if she had to. "Go!"

He didn't go immediately. Instead, Marcus grabbed a broom which was leaning in the corner and jabbed it at the light bulb. It was one of those industrial type which had a cage around it, and when he poked it, just right, the light went out, shrouding them in nothing but the dim, eerie green of the emergency lighting, but the broken glass stayed within the confines of the cage.

"There. Hopefully that will make the shutter door less conspicuous, and they'll overlook it."

With that, he climbed through the narrow opening, pulled the blonde onto his lap, and the pair of them disappeared from view.

Kayla wasted no time cramming herself through the small gap. It was a tight squeeze. Jeez, she needed to lose some weight.

She briefly worried that she might get wedged, but a particularly loud smash against the balcony door did wonders for her nimbleness. She grabbed the shutter handle and pulled it down behind her, before plummeting into the dark just as she heard the distinctive sound of a door crashing back on its hinges and the certain knowledge that the stairwell had been breached.

It wasn't quite like a slide, thank goodness. The chute narrowed and Kayla slowed as she got to the bottom, saving her from what she was convinced would have been a broken leg. Perhaps there was something to be said for the size of her ass after all. Now there was a thought!

Marcus was waiting, his phone already lighting the dank space, and helped her to her feet.

She searched in her bag for her own phone and flipped on the torch function, shining it around the walls and ceiling to see if they could find the exit.

The space was empty, so there'd be nowhere to hide if this place was discovered.

"Over here," came the muffled voice of the girl.

"I think we can open this," Marcus decided as he searched all around it with his torchlight.

Kayla didn't ask if it was safe to do so. He would have already weighed up all the pros and cons.

Thankfully, their vehicle wasn't parked in the carpark, but a block down the street, so that wasn't a concern.

She and Marcus would be able to get away without being too conspicuous, in their dark clothing, which might just as easily be nightclub wear. Kayla wasn't so sure about Marcus's sub, who looked like she was dressed in her nightie.

* * *

S hould they stay or should they leave?

The two options warred in Marcus's head. There was no way of knowing if the trapdoor was being watched. They might walk straight into an ambush.

On the other hand, if this area was revealed, they were sitting ducks. At least if they got out, even if they didn't get far, then it would be their word against the authorities that they'd ever been inside the building. If they were caught inside, there was no chance.

The trapdoor was bolted from the inside, so there was no problem getting it unlocked. The bar that secured it was stainless steel, so thankfully it hadn't rusted. He drew it open as quietly as he could, but the double doors hardly budged.

They had moved a little, though, and there had been no surge in shouting from the outside, so he figured they were relatively safe.

"Hold that light over here, so I can see what's stopping this," Marcus called to his sister. When she was in place, he pushed the doors back open, holding his breath and praying that the beams of light didn't call any attention to them. Luckily, it was dulled by the thicket of vines that enshrouded the opening.

Marcus closed it again and took stock. Anything too noisy was going to give them away.

"Your bondage shears," Kayla whispered. "Are they in your bag?"

Marcus grabbed the leather rucksack. His sister was a genius. He'd hug her if time wasn't so desperate.

Finding the sturdy shears, Marcus went about snipping through the vines, where they met at the gap between the two doors. If they did this right, the growth would just fall back into place, and they might not even leave an obvious trail that could give them away.

When he finished, he ordered all the lights out before he poked his head tentatively through the gap.

It wasn't deserted by any means. He could hear strident voices and the odd shout; the general hubbub of people close by. But there were none in the immediate vicinity. If they could get to the cover of the scrubby bit of woodland approximately ten metres away, they'd have to be given the benefit of the doubt if they were apprehended.

He climbed out first, thankful he was wearing black, then one from each side, he and the girl helped Kayla make the ungainly climb, since her clothing was also dark.

As he reached in an arm to help out the sub, once Kayla was through and on the lookout, he whispered to her, "Try to stay shielded between us two, so your clothing isn't so noticeable."

She'd gotten them this far. He'd be damned if he didn't get her the rest of the way out of here safely.

* * *

They'd made it.

Marcus breathed a sigh of relief as their hired SUV came into view. He shoved down the urge to run and slung his arm around the girl, like they were just out for a stroll, even though the windy winter weather wasn't the kind you be dressed so skimpily in. Kayla, by silent agreement, covered her back.

When they reached the car, he opened the door and gestured for her to get in.

"It okay, I can manage from here," she demurred.

This was Detroit, and not a great area. No way Marcus was allowing a half-clothed girl to wander around on her own. His personal moral compass wouldn't allow it, never mind his overdeveloped dominant personality, which insisted he always take care of a woman.

Especially this one.

"Absolutely not," he dictated. For a moment, he thought she might argue, but Kayla came to his assistance.

"He's right," she agreed. "It not safe and we can drop you anywhere. It's not a problem."

There was a long second, then she nodded and climbed in. Marcus ran around to the driver's side and jumped in, but he drove away quietly and let the night swallow them into the rest of the traffic.

They drove a few miles in silence, each of them lost in their own thoughts, until she piped up. "You can drop me here; I have a friend that lives across the road."

Marcus pulled over but stopped her from getting out immediately. "You don't have a purse or anything. Are you sure we can't take you home?"

"I don't live locally, but honestly, I'll be okay."

Marcus got out his wallet and drew out some notes, but she put her hand over his before he could give them to her.

"Don't!" she said. "I'm not a damn whore. Don't do that to me, please."

"That's not the way it is," he exclaimed. "You know that. Seriously, I can't let you out in the middle of Detroit, dressed like that and with no means of... anything on you. What sort of person does that make me?"

"I'm not your responsibility..."

Kayla reached across the middle console from the back seat with a sheaf of bills in her hand.

"Look, if the only thing that's stopping you is feeling like you're being paid for you services, then take it from me instead," she said, her own dominant personality revving full bore. "Because my brother is right. You got us out of there and that means more than you could ever possibly realise. So, call it what you like, but we owe you. The least we can do is make sure you have the means to get home safely."

The girl looked at the money, then sighed. "Okay, you're right. It will help me get home."

Marcus wondered if she really did have a friend living around here, but he couldn't exactly call her a liar. A gust of wind strong enough to make the car shudder blew across and Marcus grabbed his long wool coat off of the back seat. "Here, take this too, you'll freeze to death otherwise. No arguments this time."

She gave him a tentative smile, looked down at herself and the weather outside, which was getting steadily worse, and finally nodded. "No arguments," she agreed.

Marcus sucked in a breath, oddly reluctant to let her go. "Look, I need to give you something else..."

"It isn't necessary," she began, but he ploughed on. "It's just a card, not a bank card for anything," he said, holding it out to show her. "But it will give you access to some clubs...

decent clubs. I don't like the idea of you in some of these shady places."

"Pfft, you're a fine one to talk," she scoffed, shaking her head.

"You're right, but I'm going to be taking my own advice, and so will my sister," Marcus said, giving Kayla the side eye. "I guess it's up to you if you use it or not."

She hesitated, then took it from his outstretched hand. She shrugged into Marcus's coat, which pretty much swamped her, but at least it would keep her warm and covered.

She had the door open a crack before she turned and looked at Marcus.

"Gabriella," she said, so quietly that he couldn't hear and leaned in towards her.

"My name. It's Gabriella. Gabi," she repeated before she hopped out of the car and disappeared into the night.

Just like the angel.

Marcus wanted to laugh out loud, despite the scare they'd all just had.

"How much did you give her?" he asked Kayla when she climbed into the front seat Gabi had just vacated. He'd only seen a couple of fives.

"About a grand," his sister replied, as she buckled her seat belt. "I sandwiched some hundreds in between the small notes.

He threw her a look and a grateful smile. She'd always been the clever one.

"And you'd better hope I have Darius's number written down somewhere too, because I slipped my phone into the pocket of your coat.

Marcus frowned. "That was a bit..."

She held up her hand and interrupted him before he'd finished. "Don't worry, I wiped it clean before I did it. There's nothing incriminating on there. It was my spare phone,

83

anyway. You know I don't take my regular one to places like this."

Marcus let out a pent-up breath as he pulled away from the curb. "Yeah, and speaking of places like this, Kayla, that was the last time. We're not doing this again."

Kayla sighed. "I know. It's far too dangerous. We need to find some kind of alternative."

She looked out of the window into the blustery night.

"I'll work on it."

Dallas Johnson

"Master Dallas?" The overly sweet tones of Lexi Leigh - probably not her real name - assailed him almost before he'd gotten both feet through the door of his regular kink club.

Dallas sighed and didn't bother to correct her use of his given name. It was pointless. His face was too recognisable for him to hide behind an anonymous club name, but it still rankled when subs didn't have the decency to use it.

"Master Dallas, may I be of service to you this evening?" the sub asked hopefully, but there was an air of calculation behind her simpering smile. One he'd seen far too many times not to recognise, sadly.

"Sorry Lexi, I've already got a scene set up for this evening. Maybe next time," he told her, giving her his best conciliatory smile.

There would be no next time, but he could still be kind. There'd been a time when he had scened with her on occasion, but she had become clingy and possessive and seen their play as a forerunner to something more permanent. Dallas had decided it was better to nip that in the bud and let her down lightly, before she got overly attached, but she continued to try and wear him down. It had become annoying.

Lexi stuck out her bottom lip in an exaggerated pout and attempted to turn puppy dog eyes on him. He might have fallen for it if he hadn't seen the flash of anger and appraisal in them for a second before she employed the acting skills she desperately wanted to be recognised for, here in LA.

That was all it took to remind him that it wasn't *him* she wanted. Not that he'd ever been in any doubt, but he'd always been a sucker for that kind of forlorn dejection.

He hardened his heart. It had been used against him once too often. All she wanted from him was what his name could give her, a boost into the Hollywood spotlight. He didn't doubt for one moment that once she got what she wanted from him, she'd be hunting for the next poor sap who could further her career.

She wouldn't be the first. And, depressingly, she probably wouldn't be the last either.

Even at fifty Dallas was used to being sought after as a Dom, but, unfortunately, not always for the right reasons.

He was in good shape for his age and sported just a smattering of grey at his temples, but it blended well with his mid brown hair, which had plenty of sun-bleached highlights from the amount of time he spent in the open air. In his younger days he'd been considered a bit of a heartthrob, and as a renown pro golf champion, there weren't many people who didn't know his face.

Unfortunately, he invariably saw 'gold-digger' in the calculating eyes of most of the women who were interested in him.

It wasn't just about money. There were plenty of rich men at the club. But with him it was about celebrity as well. They wanted the media exposure as much as the money. Maybe more. And saw him as their ticket to getting it.

He'd learned that the hard way a long-ago time ago, but it had taken not one but two encounters before the lesson stuck.

Ever since, he'd steered clear of women with dollar signs in their eyes and fame in their hearts. He'd gotten pretty good at learning the tells.

Excusing himself from Lexi and pretending not to notice how much she was fuming, he went off to look for his play partner, since he hadn't been lying to her. He really did have a scene set up.

* * *

Dallas stroked his hand down the smooth, pale skin of the sub he had tied to the spanking bench and checked the rough hemp ropes he'd tied her wrists and ankles with. They weren't his preferred binding, but Sadie, the sub he was scening with, was a rather extreme masochist and liked the added chafe of this particular type of rope.

He adjusted the ball gag, another of Sadie's little foibles, and shook out a blindfold which he tied snuggly around her head.

She liked to watch the initial stages; liked to see the bindings and the gag being put on. But once the scene started, it was her preference to have her senses impaired. She said it helped her concentrate on what was happening without the external stimulus distracting her, and it was always part of her negotiations.

He stood back and looked at her, appreciating the spectacle she made, tied, as she was, by her ankles, to a spanking bench, but with her torso stretched forwards and slightly higher over a padded bar. Her generous breasts were dangling over the other side and adorned with a pair of weighted clamps.

She was beautiful in her bondage, but it was a bit too prescripted if he was honest with himself. The entire scene all about what Sadie wanted. It wasn't exactly topping from the bottom, since this was always how she negotiated things from the outset, and that was her prerogative. But it took some of the joy out of it for the Dom to be told exactly how the scene was going to play out, and many of the others refused to play with her these days.

Dallas was one of the exceptions and he had his own reasons. Sadie was young, probably young enough to be his daughter. But the one thing she was absolutely adamant about was no strings. And that meant she spoke his kind of language.

He shook off the maudlin that his run-in with Lexi had prompted and appreciated what he did have.

There was a hot woman waiting for his particular brand of dominance. And he knew just what she needed.

He started lightly with a flogger, probably *too* light for Sadie. He wasn't the sadist she needed, but the pair of them had an understanding, since he was one of the few who would accept her demands. Most Doms wanted to spin their own scenarios, within the boundaries that a submissive set up, not be told exactly what to do. It was part of the power dynamic.

Dallas wasn't the exception, just accepting.

And for whatever reasons, Sadie needed this, and being able to give her what she required assuaged some of his own needs, too. It wasn't ideal, but it was better than the alternative that subs like Lexi proffered, which came with a different set of strings attached. At least Sadie's were harmless and transparent.

When he'd heated her skin to his satisfaction so that it glowed a pale pink, he swapped out to the heavier flogger she liked. It had knots on the end, which left little round bruises.

He swung it with pinpoint accuracy from the long practice of handling a golf club and immersed himself in her enjoyment as the distinctive thuds of the flails hitting her skin had her panting and mewling in delight, the evidence of her desire coating her sleek thighs.

He preferred something tamer, himself, but he couldn't deny the visual spectacle she presented with each little splotch of red painting her skin like demon kisses.

He took care not to overdo it. He knew Sadie got as much pleasure from seeing the deviant patterns blunt force created on her skin, as she did from experiencing the stinging torment, pain slut that she was.

Dallas switched to the cane. The one he was using was particularly thin and whippy, and he lined it up just as he would a golf stroke before he pulled back his arm and laid a crisp welt of red across her buttocks.

Sadie screamed her satisfaction, curving her spine momentarily at the line of fire he rained on her eager flesh, before stretching out and wiggling her butt for more.

Four... five... six times he thrashed her pale globes. The lines crossed and intersected in a random cross-hatch pattern. Dallas would have liked to see them run like perfect ladder rungs, all equidistant apart, but this was her show.

She'd have taken more, but he had a mind to make her wait. To deviate, ever so slightly, from the script. And that was fine, too. She knew he liked to change things up. It was also part of their agreement.

Moving around in front of her, he freed his semi-stiff dick.

"Make me hard," he demanded as he removed the ball gag and shoved his shaft in her face without bothering to clean up the drool that dripped down her chin.

She stuck out her tongue eagerly, licking and laving until he was rigid enough to thrust down her throat. Then he wrapped her hair around his hands for leverage and fucked her face as she choked and gagged around his cock.

He thought there was a flash, and it made him jolt, but looking up from where his bruised and bound submissive had her lips stretched around his shaft, he saw it was just a couple using a violet wand at the next station.

"Take it, slut," he roared at Sadie, redoubling his efforts and powering into her mouth; humiliating her just the way she liked to make up for his lapse.

There were more flashes, but he ignored them, concentrating all his efforts on his submissive.

In the end, that was something that would cost him dear.

* * *

"What the actual fuck?" Dallas's voice had all the roar and growl of a wounded bear, and anyone with an ounce of sense would have given him a wide berth. But the smug looking woman who stood in front of him just smiled like the cat who'd got the cream.

Dallas had never been tempted to hit a woman before - not outside the safe, sane and consensual ethos of risk aware kink, but right now, that ethic was being sorely tested. Not that he'd ever give her any more ammunition with which to hang him by than she already had.

And she had plenty.

He swung away from Lexi and paced across the floor of his luxury penthouse, clenching and unclenching his fists and clamping his jaw closed to prevent himself from saying something ill advised, while he tried to get his head around what she'd done.

And how did she get his address? She'd knocked, then barged in when he'd opened the door and started making her demands. But his physically invaded privacy was just a small thing in comparison with the bombshell she'd just dropped.

Dallas's chest heaved, and he sucked in angry breaths between his gritted teeth. He wanted to strangle her. He wanted to put his million-dollar hands around her scrawny throat and squeeze and for that reason he crossed his arms in front of him and looked rigidly out of the floor to ceiling windows, even though nothing outside computed in his shell-shocked brain.

What the hell did he do about this?

It was blackmail. That's what this was. And right now, he was so angry that he could barely keep a lid on it.

"What do you want from me?" he finally ground out,

without turning around. He couldn't bear to look at her. Could bear to see the scheming, unscrupulous face of the bitch who undoubtedly held his future in the palm of her deceitful, conniving hand.

He was expecting some extortionate seven-digit figure, was prepared for it... but he wasn't prepared for what she asked for.

"It's simple," Lexi said, all vestiges of the sweet, simpering submissive she played at the club completely gone.

Dallas couldn't help wondering if that had all been an act, too.

"I want to be your girlfriend. I want you to wine and dine me at all the best restaurants. I want to be your plus one at all your social engagements. I want the world and the media to see me shine and being on your arm will give me the opportunity to do that."

Dallas stared at her and knew his expression must be one of complete horror. She might be accomplished at acting, but he most certainly was not. There was no way he'd be able to pull off spending any amount of time in her company without his true feelings shining through. And undoubtedly the paparazzi would pick up on that, too, since the mere thought of being near her made his skin crawl.

Damned if he did, and damned if he didn't.

His mind was whirling so fast it was making him nauseas... or maybe that was a result of the trap he'd unwittingly found himself in.

He said nothing. Couldn't have found the words even if he wanted to.

"I can see you have a lot to think about," she said with a tinkling laugh. "So, I'll just leave these here as a reminder."

She placed the package down on his glass topped coffee table.

"They're copies, of course. You can look through them and then let me know when your next social engagement is.

Make sure I have plenty of notice. I'll need time to buy something glamorous. You can let me know where you have accounts that I can charge my evening wear too, as well," she finished, twisting the knife as surely as she spun around to head back towards the door.

She stopped after she'd opened it, blowing him a kiss over her shoulder before she walked out, as bold as brass, as if she hadn't just threatened to overturn his entire world.

Dallas stood staring after Lexi for long after the lock had clicked into place behind her. Then he stumbled to a chair and collapsed into it heavily. He looked at what she'd left and tentatively reached out to pick it up.

Photos. All blown up to make the most of every visible detail.

Photos of his scene at the club with Sadie.

Out of context, they looked horrific. She was bound and bruised with cane welts across her ass. There were pictures of him administering both, then there was another of his fucking her face, but that wasn't all. There was a video too. Taken right at the time, he'd called her a slut. Something else to be taken out of context.

At least Sadie had the blindfold, so her identity was obscured to a certain extent, because this didn't just affect him if it got out, and that made it even worse.

It made him responsible for somebody else's disgrace, too.

* * *

A couple of hours later, he was even more furious. The emergency meeting with his lawyer had not gone well. The guy clearly didn't understand the intricacies of the kink lifestyle. He just looked and saw what everyone else was going to see.

"Well, if you engage in this kind of activity, I imagine it's likely to get out at some point," the guy had said.

Dallas had fired him on the spot.

The lawyer realised his mistake immediately and tried to wheedle his way back into Dallas's good graces by trying to make out that he was just reciting what other people would say. But it was too late. Dallas had seen the disgust and derision in his expression when he'd shown him a couple of the pictures... and not even the worst ones. No way someone with that attitude would be able to mount any kind of objective defence if he already thought Dallas was guilty - maybe not of actual abuse, but certainly of being one fucked up bunny.

He was in danger of wearing out his carpet. His pacing had got to such a critical level. He just couldn't keep still. His skin felt too small for his body, giving him a constant underlying urge to claw his way out of it, and as soon as he stopped moving, his thoughts overwhelmed him.

It was even worse than before. At least when Lexi had left here, he'd thought he'd got some chance of mounting a defence. His lawyer had trashed that hope with his ignorant and judgemental attitude.

Yes, Dallas could find another lawyer, but how many was he going to go through, only to find they all had exactly the same attitude before he ran out of time?

Dallas fisted his fingers into his hair and stifled the frustrated growl that was trying to escape. That's when the name of a friend who just might be able to help him popped into his head. He was a lawyer - corporate rather than personal, but surely he'd be able to recommend someone.

Thumbing through his contacts, he found the number for Logan Thornton, a Dom and shibari master, but also heavily involved in another kink club, Club Risqué.

Pressing to dial, he hoped his friend would have some good news for him.

"Hey Dallas, it's been a while," Logan's cheerful voice registered on the other end of the phone. "How are things with you? I see you cleared up at the Canadian Open. Well done."

"Thanks mate," Dallas replied. "I wish I could say things were good, but right now I really need your help."

Logan listened while Dallas told him about the situation and let out a low curse when he'd finished. "Damn, that sucks, man," he commiserated. "There are a few things you need to do straight away. First off, inform your club. An upscale establishment like yours should have non-disclosure agreements in place, so they'll likely want to mount their own legal challenge."

He paused for that information to settle in, and Dallas jotted down notes. It was good advice and something he hadn't considered while he'd been in full panic mode.

"The other thing you need to do is warn the other party," Logan continued. "I'd advise you to do that face to face and show the submissive the photos and explain the threats against you."

"Yeah, I was planning to do that," Dallas replied with a sigh. "It's not fair on her to have this coming out of the blue if the shit hits the fan."

"I'll send you the contact details of someone who'll be able to help you," Logan said, before he rang off. "She's good, and she's in the lifestyle."

Dallas breathed a sigh of relief. It was the best news he'd had all day.

* * *

Things moved quickly after that. The lawyer Logan recommended, Mia Hemmings, was way younger than Dallas expected, and also very beautiful, with her jet-black hair and startling blue eyes. But, more importantly, she clearly knew her stuff, and she didn't hang around. She set up meetings with both Dallas and Sadie straight away.

Sadie was a star. While it was true that it was more difficult to identify her, because of the mask and the way the gag distorted her features, Dallas really hadn't expected her to be so chilled about it.

Well... maybe chilled was the wrong word. She was remarkably laid back about the pictures themselves, but when it came to Lexi, boy was she mad!

"That little fucking bitch!" Sadie swore when Dallas revealed Lexi's blackmail plan. "I hope you're not giving in to that shit, that's just... wow, I can't even..."

Mia supported Sadie's general contention, but in slightly more dignified tones. "Certainly it's not a good idea for you to succumb to this kind of coercion."

"Blackmail," Sadie stated, bluntly. "Say it like it is, Counselor."

Mia sighed. "Blackmail," she agreed. "I'll be frank, Mr. Johnson, it rarely ends well, I'm afraid."

"Dallas, please," he insisted.

She inclined her head. "Unfortunately, even if you go along with all her demands, there's the likelihood she'll always hold this over you."

"You mean, when she's squeezed me for everything I'm good for on the social circuit, she'll probably move on and start demanding money," he guessed, pursing his lips.

Mia gave him a conciliatory look. "That's pretty much it, Dallas. I'm sorry."

"Well, I guess I always knew that was the most likely scenario. This is really just about damage control, isn't it?"

"Look Dallas, if Lexi spills this, then you can one hundred percent count on me to refute whatever claims she tries to make that this is abuse. Because, let's face it, we all know that's what she's angling for," Sadie said earnestly.

He reached over and squeezed her hand, giving her a small smile. "I appreciate it, Sadie, but I don't want to drag you into this mess. The way it stands, nobody ever needs to know who's in those photos with me."

He didn't say the rest of it. That if those pictures, the video, got out that no matter how much she defended him, it would have catastrophic consequences. He was a sporting individual. That meant he was essentially self-employed. He didn't work for a team, didn't have a salary. And while winning accounted for some of his income, he still had to win, and he was an old dog in an increasingly young game. While it was true, that experience counted for a great deal in a game like golf, he knew his best years were behind him, which meant he relied mostly on some very lucrative sponsorship deals. And those were the kind of thing that would dry up in the blink of an eye at the very hint of scandal.

"In the meantime, I'm going to liaise with your club, because I'm familiar with the establishment and I know they have strict rules about photography. They also have NDAs in place to prevent exactly this kind of thing from happening. Since their reputation depends on it, this isn't something that they're going to let slide," Mia continued, and Dallas appreciated her reassurance.

That was an angle Dallas was pretty certain Lexi hadn't considered. Maybe she really had expected him to just roll over and yield to her demands. But he was a Dom, and it went against his very nature to be anyone's patsy. She should know better than that. It simply wasn't in his makeup. "So, is there anything we can do to stop her?" he asked.

"Well, initially, I'd say avoid any social events you might have planned, while we get a course of action set up. That way, she can't accuse you of not following through. At least until we're more prepared to deal with it. We can apply for an injunction, but these things take time and the trouble with the sort of people who are desperate enough to do this kind of thing is that they are pretty much a loose cannon. If something triggers Ms. Leigh, she might just let fly without any thought for the consequences to herself or anyone else. She might even think there won't be any," Mia revealed, her eyebrows knitted together as she reviewed the photographs that were strewn over her desk. "And this isn't a one step, single person crime. She's already risked prosecution from the club, so that's that entire company, plus potentially the two of you on her case. If anything goes wrong, she might just feel like she has nothing to lose."

When Dallas left Mia's office fifteen minutes later, he expected to have found some modicum of relief. Instead, a feeling of foreboding crept into his bones.

* * *

Dallas spent the next two weeks living on his nerves and waiting for the other shoe to drop.

He'd cancelled all his engagements and while he'd spoken to the club to give them all the pertinent details as they mounted their own case against Lexi Leigh, he hadn't been back there since the night of the incident.

Neither had Lexi, according to his sources, but he didn't know if that was a good or a bad thing.

She hadn't contacted him again, and Dallas was torn between thinking that she'd gotten cold feet and decided against her drastic course of action and thinking that he must have missed a step and there was something he was supposed to have done. Something he'd overlooked which would have the house of cards he was currently living under falling down around his ears.

Disaster, when it came, arrived in the form of a jarring, irate phone call from his main sponsor right when he was least expecting it.

"We're cancelling your contract, you sick son of a bitch," his normally mild-mannered contact spat at him down the phone. "People like you ought to be castrated, you sick fuck."

Ice cascaded down Dallas's spine, but he played it cool. "I've no idea what you're talking about, Stan," he told the man that he'd always been on friendly terms with in the past. Apparently, that meant nothing in the light of scandal.

"Then google it. You're trending, you filthy animal, and not in a good way."

Dallas swore under his breath and grabbed his phone. He didn't even need to search; the wonders of the worldwide web were already inundating him with suggestions for posts where he could see the very worst of himself in a grim and ugly lack of context.

"This isn't what it looks like, Stan. Honestly." He hated the pleading quality evident in his voice, but apparently none of that meant anything either.

"I don't care what it looks like. I don't even care if someone pasted your head on someone else's body. You think we want that kind of perversion linked with a wholesome name like ours? I can tell you right now, we want the full return of all payments made, and we'll be looking for compensation for the tarnishing of our image."

"Now wait a minute," Dallas argued. "I've worked with you for almost a decade. You surely can't be suggesting I'm liable for contracts already served and expired."

"That's exactly what I'm saying. You think we want any kind of association with your sordid mess, Johnson? I don't give a flying fuck what the story is. I don't even give a shit if you're the victim of some kind of Photoshop scam. All I'm interested in is protecting our good name."

Stan continued his rant, but Dallas zoned him out as all the blood drained from his face and he started to feel numb. He couldn't believe his sponsor wasn't interested in the truth.

"I'll have my lawyer contact you," he said to the man on the other end of the phone before he cut him off.

And that was only the tip of the iceberg. Charging him from every direction were furious people whose only intention was to make sure the muck landed as far away from them as possible.

Not just companies and sponsors, but individuals too. Colleagues who he had considered friends, people he'd been out to dinner with, laughed with and socialised with, all suddenly turned on him like he was some kind of pariah.

In the end, he turned his phone off, but not until he'd spoken to Mia and checked on Sadie. As much as he wanted to crawl into a hole and stay there until the world stopped going mad, he at least owed them that much.

"I'm so sorry, Dallas," Mia's husky voice was genuinely empathetic. At least one person wasn't blasting at him, but she also didn't have good news. "Unfortunately, Ms Leigh released everything anonymously, so any kind of recourse will be that much more difficult."

"How can it be difficult?" Dallas asked, though in reality he was already feeling defeated. He'd be lucky if he wasn't bankrupted when this was over. Already, the sheer volume of animosity towards him was overwhelming.

"Well, early indications show that her name isn't linked to any of this. Even the original upload site is an IP address of a cybercafe. We've already checked and there's no security feed footage and no one matching her description was there when it was uploaded." Mia explained the technical stuff, and Dallas listened in silence.

"The email address used was closed down as soon as the content had been shared a couple of times and it was out in the public domain. Tracing it back to her is going to be hard. She can just claim that somebody else did it."

Dallas massaged his forehead. He had a headache of biblical proportions and he already knew that the scandal which had become his life wasn't going to abate any time soon.

"Surely she must be culpable, since she took the photos and video and threatened to blackmail me with it," he replied quietly, rubbing both his hands over his face. He felt sick and out of control and he hated it, but that wasn't even the worst of the three-ring circus that was going on around him.

"And that's what we'll argue," Mia told him. "But..." She paused and sighed.

"But what?" Dallas demanded, bracing himself for more bad news.

"Well, it's her word against yours unless we can find someone at the club who's willing to come forward as a witness. Sadie doesn't really count since she's in the photographs and it can be argued that she's too scared to tell the truth. And the likelihood is that..."

"... Anyone who might have that kind of information won't want to be identified," Dallas finished for her.

And he didn't blame them. Why the hell would anyone want to throw themselves on this bonfire?

"I'll do what I can, Dallas," Mia said softly.

And she would. He knew she would.

But it might not be enough to stop everything he'd ever worked for from crashing and burning and turning to ash at his feet.

* * *

S adie's response was completely different.

"That scheming bitch is going to pay," she ranted, and Dallas had to move the receiver away from his ear.

"I'm sorry you've been caught up in all this," he apologised. At least her name didn't appear anywhere. The one small mercy in all of this was that she'd retained her anonymity. He couldn't have lived with himself if he'd pulled someone else into this mess.

She was quiet for a moment and Dallas wondered if he was going to feel the sharp lash of her tongue, along with those that had already cut him.

He wouldn't blame her. If there was one person who was justified in being angry with him, then it was Sadie. She'd been thrown into the middle of this seething vortex through no fault of her own.

He should think about compensating her. She was the one person he'd be glad to it for. Especially if her name finally came out. He opened his mouth to say so, but she spoke before he could put it out there.

"I don't blame you for this, Dallas," she said, seriously. "You're just as much a victim in all this. More, really. Even if my name gets out, I don't have anything to lose, not like you do. But believe me, Lexi Leigh is not going to get away with this. Not if I have anything to do with it."

* * *

S adie Smith put the phone down after speaking to Dallas and narrowed her eyes at the video that was playing on her laptop.

She hadn't been kidding when she'd told him Lexi was going to pay. That conniving bitch might have thought she'd covered her tracks, but she'd messed with the wrong person.

She'd taken something beautiful and precious and goddamn *private* and thrown it out for the world and his dog to bat around, sharing and circulating it while they spread their pious judgement.

Sadie wasn't the type to get mad. She saved her energy for getting even. She'd learned at a young age to make the best of your lot in life and make it work for you. It was why she was the way she was.

Detached.

Aloof.

Broken.

But now she was an adult, no one got to hurt and humiliate her without her explicit consent.

Sadie had vowed that she would never be a victim again, and Lexi Leigh had put her back into that position.

That was unforgivable, in Sadie's book.

She didn't wait. She didn't stop or second guess her actions. She didn't change her clothes or bother with any primping. She was perfectly calm.

She grabbed one important item before leaving her tiny apartment to hunt Lexi Leigh down.

Sadie had no acting aspirations herself. But she'd learned a lot about what people expected and how behaving a certain way might be advantageous. It was a skill that had aided her many times when she was a kid.

But she hadn't expected to be using them again.

She hammered on the door, making as much noise as she possibly could. "How could you do this to me, Lexi?" she sobbed loudly, on the other side of the threshold. Lexi lived in a busy tower block and there were plenty of people around. Sadie used it to her advantage.

"The club is supposed to be a safe place, but you..."

She didn't need to say any more before Lexi threw open the door, looked both ways to see who was listening, then grabbed Sadie's arm and yanked her inside.

"Jeez, be careful what you're saying. People might hear!"

"Seriously Lexi? Why the hell would I be worried about that when you just released a video of me and Dallas which is now all over the internet?"

Just as she had calculated, Lexi didn't waste time asking what she was talking about or how Sadie knew it was her. She was too intent on moving the train wreck Sadie represented out of public sight.

Lexi exhaled impatiently. "None of this was about you, S..."

"Really?" she interrupted. "Because it feels a lot like it's about me the way people are sharing that video, and judging me, and assuming that I'm being abused. Why Lexi? Why would you do that to me? Video me and take photos in a place that's supposed to be safe. Where we have to sign NDAs, so this kind of things doesn't happen. What have I ever done to you to deserve this?"

"For god's sake, honestly, it wasn't about you, it was about Dallas. I just wanted to use it as a bit of leverage," Lexi told her bluntly. "I needed his connections to get my foot up in Hollywood."

Sadie put on a pathetic whimper. If Lexi knew her better, she might have realised it was fake. "You did all this just to get yourself noticed?" she asked. "What? And I just got caught in the crossfire? My kinks, my pleasures, my private pursuits, you deliberately caught on camera and put out there for the world to view, all because you wanted to be seen? Why didn't you just get someone to film one of your own kink scenes?"

"Don't be stupid," Lexi replied scornfully, flicking her artfully styled hair over one shoulder. Her whole attitude was less than sympathetic. Like she couldn't care less about who she trampled on and hurt to get her own way. "The idea was that I would be Dallas Johnson's girlfriend and he would take me to all the places I needed to be to rub shoulders with the kind of people I need to cosy up to."

"You... you mean you were b-blackmailing him?" Sadie asked, adding a good dose of shock to her voice.

"Ha! Hardly. I never even got that far..."

"But... then why did you release all this to the media then?"

"Because I was tipped off about the club taking legal action." Lexi revealed, pacing back and forth.

"What? That makes no sense. You'd have been better off keeping it quiet, Lexi." Sadie deliberately repeated the other girl's name every chance she got.

"That bastard obviously told them I'd taken unauthorised photos and video inside the club. He needed to pay," she replied viciously, her face contorted into an ugly mask of venomous intentions.

Sadie was specific in how she worded everything. Luckily, Lexi was too wrapped up in her own perceived outrage to notice. "There's CCTV all over the club, Lexi. You know that. It's for our protection; to make sure nothing happens that isn't completely *consensual*. They probably caught you! So why the hell would you throw me to the wolves just because the club is going to take action because you broke a legally binding non-disclosure agreement? That makes no sense."

"Like I keep repeating, none of this was about you," Lexi told her, like that made everything all right.

"What, so I was just collateral damage while you were throwing your toys out of the playpen for getting caught doing something you shouldn't?" Sadie reigned in her attitude, realising anger was getting the better of her. It wouldn't do for Lexi to notice she wasn't quite as pathetic as she made out.

"This is my *life*, Lexi, and you just threw me out there to vultures. Dallas too. He's a nice man. Neither of us deserved any of this." She added a pitiful sniffle to her words for effect.

"Oh, for pity's sake. Suck it up, you pathetic cretin. No one can tell it's you with the gag distorting your features and that blindfold on." Lexi's entire attitude was one of malicious vitriol, clearly proving to anyone that she didn't about anyone but herself. She'd probably sell her own grandmother if it got her a step up in the world.

Sadie shot her a last baleful look. She'd got everything she needed. Just one last cherry on the cake.

"Seriously? And that makes it all right? You really are something, Lexi Leigh."

Sadie twirled away and let herself out of Lexi's flat. She ran and didn't look back. Let Lexi think it was out of despair. That girl was about to get her comeuppance.

She didn't even wait to get home before she uploaded the video to an anonymous account before posting it online and covering her tracks.

Lexi Leigh was about to find out just what it felt like to have your privacy invaded and nobody deserved it more.

Let's see how this footage improved her chances in Hollywood. Sadie was pretty sure no one would touch her with a ten foot pole after this.

Payback really was a bitch.

* * *

Sadie wasn't surprised to find Dallas on her doorstep later that evening. He didn't say anything when she let him in, just pulled her into a conciliatory hug, which she allowed for a few seconds. She didn't particularly like being touched like this.

"Are you okay?" Dallas asked. He really was a nice man. One of the better ones.

"I'm good," she replied, honestly, pulling away to pour two mugs of coffee from the machine in her tiny kitchen. "Really, I am."

Dallas nodded. He knew her better than most people.

"I sent copies of the original video to the club and to your lawyer," she told him as she set the mugs down on the coffee table in front of him.

"Yeah, Mia told me," he replied, his arms resting on his thighs and dangling between his knees.

He looked haggard, like he'd aged overnight. All this had taken its toll on him, and Sadie knew better than to think that what she'd done was some kind of magic wand that would automatically make everything better.

Shit stuck. That was the sad truth, and it didn't matter whether you deserved it or not.

Hopefully, though, it would at least put to bed the insinuation that he abused women, when nothing could be further from the truth.

"The police are questioning her now and the club has rescinded her membership and circulated her details to all the other reputable BDSM establishments," Dallas informed her.

"And what about you, Dallas?" she asked tentatively, picking up her coffee and taking a sip.

Dallas followed her lead and grabbed his own mug, nursing it between both hands as he looked off into the distance of his mind, a resigned look on his face. "Mia's done one hell of a job at damage control," he revealed. "One fuck up and people think they can reclaim everything they ever paid you, never mind that you worked your ass off for it way back when."

There was a bitterness in his voice and the acceptance that he'd lost more than mere money and reputation. He'd lost people who he'd considered friends over this, and Sadie felt for him. She knew what it was like to be let down by the people who were supposed to be there for you.

"Mia's managed to get the liability restricted to current contracts only and negotiate compensation down to the repayment of the balance of the contract." He gave a bitter laugh and stared into his coffee cup. "Half of them will still have the audacity to use the advertisements that have already been made, regardless. You know what they say. No publicity is bad publicity."

He snapped himself out of it and looked back at her. "Is there anything I can do for you, Sadie? You really did get caught in the crossfire on this one. Just say the word and I'll write you a cheque."

Sadie held up her hand to stop him. "No way. None of this is your fault, Dallas, and you're already haemorrhaging cash like someone attacked your wallet with a knife and left multiple stab wounds. If anyone should be compensating me, it should be that bitch, Lexi. This is all down to her. Or even the club. Despite what I said to Lexi, I know there's no CCTV footage, I just said that to throw her off. But none of the Dungeon Monitors saw what was going on. They said the room was too dark, which I guess is fair enough. But Lexi just taking pictures like that? Well, it should never have been allowed to happen."

"It's a wake-up call for them, that's for sure," Dallas agreed. "They'll need to do a lot to make members feel secure again. Do yourself a favour, though, and at least negotiate yourself a couple of years free membership."

"You make it sound like you're not going to be there," Sadie acknowledged sadly.

Dallas gave her a humourless smile. "I'll be around for a while, but I've been given an investment opportunity that I'm hoping to negotiate into a full-time job. It's time for me to quit the circuit. There's a whole horde of young, talented players poised to replace me, and without sponsorship, I'll just be paying to play. Might as well go somewhere I'm valued and not going to be the butt of a bunch of narrow-minded ridicule."

He stood with a grace that belied his years and took something from his jacket pocket.

"If I can ever do anything for you, Sadie, just get in touch." He handed her a card with his details on it. "I mean it. That's an open-ended offer. Whether it's next week, next year, or ten years time, I'll do what I can to help you. That's a promise you can rely on."

Sadie stared at the matt black business card and stroked her thumb over the shiny raised print, before she nodded and tucked it carefully into her pocket.

"I'll see you around," he told her as he headed for the door. He turned to her before he left and dropped a brief kiss on her forehead, which, for some reason, made her want to cry.

"Take care of yourself," she murmured as he took his leave.

Looking after him, Sadie couldn't help but wonder if she'd ever cross paths with Dallas Johnson again.

Ash Millington

Trigger Warning: This story contains bereavement.

Ash Millington

"Why don't you let me take you to the club. Just once," Ash wheedled, kissing Jenny's fingers. "Just so you can get a feel for it before you make up your mind."

Jenny snatched her hand away like he'd burned her and threw him a derisive look. "No!" she replied decisively. "I don't know how many times I've told you; I don't want to visit that perverted place. And what do you need to go there for, anyway? We're married. Am I not enough for you?"

She knew exactly what to say to put him on a guilt trip.

"You know I would never dream of going without you, pet. I just thought it might be something we could explore together." He tried again, even though it wasn't the first time he'd tried to have this discussion. She'd always managed to divert the conversation in the past, so it had never been concluded. Had that been deliberate? He'd like to think she could at least be open minded about his own persuasions. Enough at least to try it before she dismissed it out of hand.

But with the next words out of her mouth, he wondered if maybe he was hoping for too much.

"And don't call me pet. It's offensive. What do you think I am, a dog or something?"

Ash reigned in his annoyance. He might be a dominant, but consent was key in the lifestyle he'd enjoyed before his marriage to Jenny, so instead he tried a different tactic. "How about we try it at home then, if you'd prefer something a little more private?" he asked hopefully.

"Look Ash," she finally said, with a huff in her voice. "I've tried to be subtle or to avoid this conversation, but you just don't give up, do you?"

"Of course not, it's important to me. It's part of who I am. You knew that when we first started dating, but you said you weren't ready and I respected that," he reminded her. "And besides, you said once we'd settled into our relationship, we could revisit this. Well, since we're married now, I think things are pretty settled, don't you?"

Jenny pulled a face that looked like she'd been sucking on a lemon. "Well, I'm sorry, but I don't want to," she said bluntly. "I've always thought it was really quite depraved, and that hasn't changed."

Ash narrowed his eyes and stared at her, so many of his emotions feeling like they'd just taken a direct hit. He swallowed past the bad taste in his mouth. "So, what you're saying is that you were just humouring me all along, it that it?"

Her silence spoke volumes, and Ash had to walk away before he did something they both regretted. Right now, he felt like he'd been used; like she'd led him on under false pretences.

It probably wasn't intentional. They were in love with each other, after all.

But right now, all he wanted to do was spank her so hard that she couldn't sit down for a week for playing him like a fool. For promising something she had no intention of keeping.

But he didn't have her permission for that.

And it was as much his fault as hers. He should have pinned her down to this conversation before they got married, instead of always allowing her to put it off, so he only had himself to blame.

He took a deep breath. It would be fine. He'd learn to accept things the way they were, and maybe one day she'd have a change of heart.

* * *

That had been five years ago. Nothing much had changed in the status quo, but they were happy for the most part. He'd learned to live with the itch that existed just underneath his skin. The one that cried out to be scratched by immersion in the kink lifestyle. Because they were a couple and couples compromised.

That was no compromise, the devil on his shoulder hissed. *You just curled up and let her walk all over you.*

Ash clenched his jaw and shut that shit down. He couldn't make her want it just because he did, and they'd taken vows for better or for worse. This might come under the marginally worse category, but he could live with it.

Or without it, in this case.

The fact that those thoughts were fresh in his head when Jenny dropped her newest bombshell probably didn't help, though.

"I want to start a family," she announced out of the blue. They'd just sat down to dinner, and he was looking forward to it because she'd made all his favourites. Maybe it wasn't out of the blue after all.

Ash paused with his fork halfway to his mouth and looked at her through narrowed eyes. Then he took the bite and finished it determinedly before her answered. "We've discussed this," he reminded her. "We have a plan."

"I don't like the plan. I want a baby now," she whined, throwing him a pouting scowl that just made him want to spank her. Again.

Not gonna happen.

"Jenny, we had a very long and in-depth discussion about this, and you agreed. It wasn't like I threw down an ultimatum which you were forced to accept. It was your decision too. You said you weren't ready to start a family."

"Well, I've changed my mind. I'm not getting any younger, you know!"

"You'll be the age you were always going to be when we agreed to start a family. You didn't think it was too old then," he retorted irritably.

"Well, that was then," she said petulantly, as if that one remark explained it all.

Ash huffed out a breath. The dinner he'd been looking forward to no longer quite so appetising. "Look Jenny, I was very clear on my reasons for wanting to put off starting a family. I work a lot of long hours, and I want to be in a position where I can wind it down and spend more time at home once the baby arrives."

"That makes no sense. We have plenty of money," she argued, stabbing at the food on her plate, but not eating it.

Ash shook his head. She had no idea. He tried for patience and set about trying to explain. "We have plenty of money, because I earn it by putting in a lot of long hours. If I reduce my hours, we'll have to cut back and a baby alone costs plenty."

"Of course, we don't need to do that. You can just carry on working your usual hours and support us in the manner we're accustomed to." Jenny reasoned. She might have been going for cajoling, but it just made Ash see red.

He threw his fork down onto his plate with a clatter, all pretence of eating forgotten. "Seriously?" he demanded, pushing his chair back so that it ground along the floor with a grating sound. "That's your answer to this?"

"What?" Jenny asked, and she looked genuinely confused, which somehow made it even worse. Like she didn't have the first idea why he might want the financial security to work less. Hell, maybe she didn't. Maybe she was so wrapped up in her own little world that his own wants and needs didn't come into it. They sure as hell hadn't when he'd wanted to discuss the kink lifestyle with her, he thought bitterly.

"It might not have occurred to you, but when we have children, I want to be around enough to actually be a part of their lives. And that isn't going to happen while I'm working fourteen-hour days six days a week."

"Why is always about what you want?" she screamed at him, leaning forward to get in his face before she slumped back in her chair and allowed fat tears to well in her eyes.

He wasn't moved by it. Not this time. She had a habit of turning on the waterworks when she wanted her own way. Ash was pretty much inured to it by now.

Instead of caving, like he normally did, he got up off the chair and shot her an icy look. "I'm sorry, Jenny, but this is too important to me to just give in to you. I want to spend time with my child too, so we'll have to stick to the plan. It's not like it's unreasonable, and you already agreed to it."

She sniffled, and he walked away. Not because he was upset by her crying, but because he was so damn angry at her selfishness. Where the heck did she get off expecting him to work all hours and miss out on his own child growing up, just to support her extravagant spending habits?

* * *

Ash was stoic six months later, when Jenny nervously told him she was pregnant. This should have been one of the most joyful moments of his life, and the two of them should be celebrating, but the circumstances left everything tarnished and tainted.

"I don't know how it happened," she wailed, dipping her head so she didn't have to look at him when he said precisely nothing at all, while her easy tears poured from her eyes.

What could he say?

It wasn't like he didn't want children; he did. But the time wasn't right. He wanted to be in a position where he could slow down and enjoy his children; spend time with them and be an active, involved parent.

This was not it and now he was just going to have to suck it up and make peace with the fact that he'd either have to forego the long-term financial security that he'd wanted to achieve before the started a family or spend less time than he wanted with his child.

Both options sucked.

"Say something," Jenny whispered, wringing her hands.

Ash just shrugged. "What is there to say? I need to get to work. I'll probably be even later than usual for a few months, while I try to get some investments in place that will allow me to spend time with my child."

He walked out of the door to the sound of her sniffling behind him. It brought back a strange sense of déjà vu.

He sucked in a deep, bracing breath as he walked to his car and tried to get his racing thoughts under control.

It wasn't Jenny's fault. She had never wanted to be on the pill. She didn't like the idea of filling her body with any kind of drugs or medication. She was a bit of a health nut and he'd always admired that about her.

Of course, that meant that contraception was his department. They always used a condom, without fail. One of the damn things must have bust.

That was an act of God and not something he should be taking out on Jenny.

Once he adjusted to the idea, everything would be fine. He had some options for 'make money quick' schemes, and he had the means to invest in them. Mostly his job involved investing other people's money, and he was a bit of a whizz at it, netting large gains for his clients. Obviously, he put his experience to good use with his own finances. But he'd been concentrating on building a long-term portfolio. Something that would last a lifetime, and he'd been putting in the hours now, so he could reap the benefits later.

All that had changed with this curve ball life had thrown at him, and if he wanted to have the opportunity to spend any time at all with this new baby, then he needed to take some bigger risks.

As he drove to work, he made a plan.

* * *

Ash took one look at the little bundle of pink and instantly fell in love. Carys, as they'd agreed to name a baby girl, resembled a prune. Her skin was wrinkled and red and covered in greasy patches of white, which he was assured was normal. Her eyes were scrunched closed and her mouth almost comically wide open as her raw scream announced her presence to the new world into which she'd been delivered.

Ash had never seen anything so beautiful in his entire life.

He was astounded at the way this tiny, wriggling parcel of newness could appear in his heart and fill up his soul so instantly. It was like magic.

And he had made this. She was a little part of him. He had created a new life, full of joy and possibilities. It was awe-inspiring and amazing, and he couldn't believe how ridiculously proud and euphoric he felt.

All the excruciatingly long days and seven-day weeks that had led up to her birth had been worth it.

Yes, it had been a strain, both mentally and physically, and hadn't helped the gulf that had sprung up between him and Jenny with her unexpected pregnancy, but that was all in the past now.

He'd made some risky investments in crypto currency. Small ones at first, while he got the feel for the market. He resolutely turned every penny he had used to its original investment and only used the profit he'd made from various deals to reinvest, so he was guaranteed never to be worse off than when he'd started.

Then, he'd seen a trend and taken the biggest gamble of his life. It wasn't something he normally would have done, but his child's impending birth and the overwhelming desire to be free to spend time with his new baby spurred him to take a calculated risk.

He took every penny of the substantial profit he'd already made and put it all into bitcoin. He watched the stats like a hawk; had them constantly running on a second screen while he did the rest of his work. He had audible alerts set up to notify him to every shift in the market, night, or day.

He hovered and twitched and lived on his nerves while he watched his investment soar, then sometimes dip a few points, then take off again. It was a game of cat and mouse, and not one for the faint hearted. Not with the amount he had invested. He couldn't lose... he didn't think. There was already enough gain to make him a ridiculously rich man, even if he cashed in now. But he stayed the course and kept his trigger finger off the sell button, allowing instinct and his knowledge of the market to guide him.

And then he got out - at exactly the right time. The market peaked, he withdrew tens of millions, and when it dropped to an all-time low, he even reinvested a couple of million, knowing he could afford for that money to just sit there until the market regained its footing. It might take a while, but that didn't matter now that his gamble had paid off, and he had enough to stop work and still support his growing family for the foreseeable future.

It was a relief.

And gazing at Carys, who was now content in his arms and looking around with blinking grey eyes, he was glad he'd made that gamble.

Crossing to Jenny and laying Carys down in her arms, he stroked her sweat slicked hair and kissed her forehead.

"Well done, sweetheart," he whispered.

Everything was going to be alright.

* * *

The first months at home with a new baby were a revelation.

Ash was glad he was able to be at home twenty-four seven to help out, because Jenny seemed to be struggling.

But that was fine. She'd spent nine months carrying his child and brought Carys into the world on a tide of pain and exhaustion he couldn't even comprehend, so he was happy to pick up the slack. He even encouraged her to express her breast milk, so he could take the night feeds and allow Jenny to catch up with some much-needed rest.

He loved those quiet times in the middle of the night when it was just him and Carys. Yes, he was tired too, but it was worth every moment of broken sleep and every exhausted nap stolen during the day.

He just wished Jenny were as enthusiastic as he was. He knew hormones played a huge part in the aftermath of birth and that baby blues could be a thing. He'd made a point of reading everything he could in the free time he had between taking care of Carys, so he was aware of all the pitfalls.

But he still thought it was sad that Jenny wasn't enjoying the baby she'd been so desperate to have.

He'd speak to the doctor. She deserved to enjoy these early days with their baby. He didn't want her to look back with regret at having missed time that could never be recovered.

* * *

Post-natal depression, the professionals said.

Ash had got Jenny help pretty early on, but her interest in the baby didn't seem to have increased at all.

Carys was six months old, and Jenny had jumped at the chance to wean her as soon as it possible. Almost like she'd been counting the days.

Ash didn't mind carrying the extra load. This time he had with his daughter was precious. He just wished Jenny wasn't missing it.

He was taking Carys for her routine six-month wellness check-up today, and Jenny was adamant she wasn't going with him.

She said she had better things to do.

Ash tried not to be angry. He knew she was struggling, but what could be more important that their child's development?

Perhaps he could ask the doctor about Jenny while he was there. See if there was more that could be done to help her.

Carys was a delight, like usual. She was such as easy child. Happy and gurgling and banging her new favourite toy, a bunny shaped rattle, on anything that would make it jangle.

"She's developing normally, and everything is right on track," the paediatric nurse told him after Carys had been weighed and measured.

She flipped to a chart in a little booklet with Carys's details on and pointed to the dots she'd scribed on it. "This is her weight, and as you can see, it's exactly where it should be."

They traded information for a while. It was the first time he'd seen the book. He hadn't known it existed until the nurse had asked for it and he'd found it in the side pocket of the baby bag.

Now he poured over it with interest. All Carys's milestones were in here. The first time she smiled. The date she started sleeping through the night. When she first started to sit up, unaided. Her first solid foods. They weren't in Jenny's handwriting, so he guessed they must have filled in during her checks. Why had he ever known about this?

Then something caught his eye, which had him confused. "Is this her blood type?" he asked, his brows knitting at the notation that couldn't possibly be right.

The nurse leaned over and looked at the entry, then pressed a couple of buttons on her PC so she could look in up on her digital records.

Ash already knew they'd made a mistake when they'd handwritten it into the little book. But that was okay. He could get her to correct it while he was here.

"Yes, that's right," she replied, finally. "A positive."

The blood in Ash's veins felt like it had suddenly run cold.

"I was expecting her to be an O blood group," he said in a voice which seemed like it came from far away. "Like mine."

"Ah, well..." the nurse nodded in understanding. "Although O is the most common blood group, A is actually the dominant type. In A/O parents, the child will always be an A."

Ash picked up Carys and got her ready to leave, somewhat mechanically.

He left the building and drove home on autopilot.

When he parked in the driveway, he realised he didn't remember a single second of the entire journey.

He did everything he needed to do by rote. Got Carys fed and changed and put her down for a nap.

Jenny wasn't home. Perhaps that was just as well. It would give him time to calm down and discuss things with her without flying off the handle.

Or perhaps it just gave him more time to stew.

More time for his mind to stray to all the bad places he didn't want to acknowledge.

He knew how genetics worked.

He knew a child would have one or the other blood group belonging to its parents.

And he also knew that Jenny was O positive, the same as him.

* * *

Ash stared at Jenny when she finally came through the door an hour later.

"Sorry," she called. "I was longer than I expected."

He looked at the multitude of shopping bags she dragged through the door. So many she was having trouble carrying them all.

"You ducked out of your daughter's check-up so you could go shopping?" he asked, another layer of disbelief adding to those already squeezing his heart.

Jenny huffed and immediately went on the defensive. "God, Ash, it was only a routine thing, it's not like I was missing anything. Besides, I thought you'd like to do it, and I had to buy Carys some new clothes. She's growing out of everything."

Carys didn't need any new clothes. Ash knew that because he was mostly the one who dressed her.

"So, what did you get her then?" he asked, his eyes narrowing on the quantity of designer label packaging, all of them from stores which he was damn sure didn't carry baby items.

"Good grief, give me a moment, would you!" Jenny exclaimed. "I've had an exhausting day."

Ash eyed her critically. It looked like she'd had her hair done, and her nails were long and elegant, sporting some intricate design.

And also, totally inappropriate for taking care of a baby. They looked like bloody talons.

He recognised one of the bags as an exclusive health spa. Couldn't have been too exhausting then, he thought with uncharacteristic bitterness.

"A funny thing happened today at the clinic," he told her

conversationally, following her into the bedroom where she took all her purchases.

She barely seemed to be taking any notice as she pulled out a couple of expensive face creams and some designer makeup. "Uh-huh," she replied, non-committal.

"Mmm..." He hardly wanted to put his suspicions into words, because that would make them real... except they were already real. He had irrefutable proof.

He clenched his jaw and forced the words out. "Yes. The nurse showed me Carys's development booklet. She has an A positive blood type."

Jenny removed a froth of satin and lace underwear from a bag and somewhere in the recesses of his mind, Ash wondered if those were for her to wear for Carys's father - her biological father.

Involuntarily, his hands tightened into fists.

Finally, Jenny seemed to sense that something was off. She stopped what she was doing and looked at him for the first time since she'd returned from her trip. She hadn't even bothered to go check on the baby, he thought, idly.

"Are you alright?" she asked with a frown.

"No," Ash grated, pinning her with a furious stare. "I've been trying to work out why Carys doesn't have my blood type."

Her eyes widened and every drop of colour seemed to leech from her face. "Well... there's an... an obvious explanation."

Her eyes skittered away from his in a revealing tell. "Sh-she must have my blood type instead," Jenny stammered.

Ash nodded slowly, and she almost seemed to wilt with relief. "That is the most obvious answer, of course," he agreed and watched as Jenny let out the breath she was holding and returned to her shopping haul like she was off the hook.

"Except you have the same blood group as me, Jenny, and

Carys is different from both of us. She is type A, which she must have inherited from her *real* father."

Those final two words left his lips on a low, bitter growl.

Jenny froze, her breathing beginning to saw in and out, fast. "It's not what you think," she whispered, desperation seeping into her already unsteady voice.

"Really?" Ash scoffed, incredulously. "Because I'm having trouble thinking of any other scenarios."

She collapsed onto the bed, head down, and picked nervously at her fingers. "I wanted a baby," she murmured so quietly he could barely hear her. He refused to step closer, though. Could hardly bear to be near her right now.

"A baby you barely bother with," he pointed out, and she flinched.

He didn't care if it was harsh. It was true. Today was a case in point. She'd proven that going out shopping and getting her hair and nails done was more important than her child. She could have done all that any day of the week, and he would happily have taken care of Carys.

But no, she had to go do it the one day their child - *her* child - had an appointment. It didn't matter if it was routine. It was the principal.

"It's not as much fun as I thought it would be," she said in a small voice, her head down still.

Something inside Ash snapped.

"Fun!" he bellowed. "*Fun? In what world did you ever think having a baby was going to be fun?*" he asked incredulously. "Having a baby is hard work. It's a responsibility. Yes, it's rewarding and enjoyable too, and when they're older, you get to do a lot of great things together, but if your idea of having a baby revolved solely around having *fun,* then no wonder you're disillusioned. She's not a damn doll, for fuck's sake!"

He sucked in a noisy breath. "And that is *not* the point.

You wanted a baby, and I said we should wait and stick to the plan - which clearly was the right thing to do - and you did what exactly?"

Fat tears were running down her face now, but Ash was unmoved. He'd been manipulated by too many of her crocodile tears in the past.

"I went to a fertility clinic and found a sperm donor. There was no other man, I promise. I haven't been unfaithful."

Incredulity roared through him, and his fragile emotions erupted with the force of a grenade going off.

"And you think that makes it all right?" Ash thundered. "You didn't get your own way, so you went behind my back. You forced me to work every hour of the day in order to get ahead so I could take some time off to spend with my family and then you literally left me holding the baby. A baby that's not even mine!"

In the connecting room, Carys started to wail and Ash felt a moment of guilt that his shouting had disturbed her. But damn it, he had to vent his anger somehow, or he might end up putting his fist through the wall.

Jenny looked from the nursery to Ash. "Aren't you going to..." She trailed off under his disbelieving glare.

"No, I am not." He wasn't in the right frame of mind to deal with a baby right now. "I suggest *you* go and look after *your* child," he sneered derisively.

For a moment, he actually thought Jenny was just going to sit there and let the baby cry. Then she bit her lip, looked at him from the corner of her eye and finally got up to do it when she realised he really wasn't going to.

Unbelievable!

She came back a few minutes later with Carys quiet but her lip was still juddering with every other breath.

It hurt to look at her; this baby he'd felt so much love and joy for.

The baby who wasn't his.

He fisted his hands reflexively and ground his teeth together.

His heart felt like it had been carelessly crumpled up inside his chest and then pounded on with giant hands until it quaked and bled.

His head was hammering, and his breaths felt they were having to be physically yanked out from inside him. His chest was so tight.

He stared at Jenny like she was a stranger. Christ, maybe she was. He sure as hell didn't know the woman who was standing in front of him with a child who taunted him with her very presence.

He couldn't bear to look at them.

To see them was to see betrayal; up close and personal. He didn't have the capacity to be composed about this right now.

"Get out of my sight, Jenny," he said. His voice quivered with the restraint he was forcing into it.

"D-don't be hasty, Ash," she replied, her voice shaky whisper. "We should talk about this like sensible adults."

His eyes flashed with renewed rage. "There have been plenty of times when I wanted to talk about our relationship, Jenny," he replied. The guttural tone was harsh. "But now is not one of them, so get out of my sight before I say something I'll regret."

She looked alarmed. Maybe she thought he was going to throw her out. Maybe she thought she'd be forced to look after the baby by herself.

Truth was, he didn't know what he was going to do right now.

He needed to think; to get his head around everything that

had happened and decide if he could come to terms with it. And he couldn't do that while she was here.

She slammed out of the front door, with the baby in tow, like she was the injured party and Ash collapsed onto the sofa in the living room and closed his eyes.

His ears were ringing from the sudden silence in the wake of the storm that had just capsized his life as he knew it.

For a while, the thoughts in his head just scrambled around in circles like they were caught in a whirlwind, and he sat there, blankly, allowing them to chase each other until gradually the most important ones coalesced.

Carys; none of this was her fault. She was still the same child he loved and took care of. The thought of losing her caused just as much pain as if she was his own. That baby had been his life for the past six months.

But where did he stand?

Biologically, she wasn't his. Did that mean he had no kind of claim over her? The blood ran cold in his veins at the thought.

No matter what happened, that little girl was the daughter of his heart and would fight for her if he had to.

His name was on the birth certificate. Surely that had to mean something.

Jenny was a different matter. A distance had grown between them since she'd told him she was pregnant.

Some of it was his fault. He'd worked long, hard hours to get them to a place of financial stability, but he would never regret that. It had given him the opportunity to take this last six months off work and he was glad about that. Especially since Jenny had been almost incapable, whether for medical reasons or just plain disinterest, of looking after Carys.

Since Carys had been born, he'd hoped to make up some of the ground that had been lost. He'd been careful and attentive. He'd shouldered the burden of childcare so Jenny could recover, but in retrospect, perhaps some of her disinterest was his fault too. Perhaps he should have made her spend time looking after the baby, instead of always allowing her to duck out of her responsibility. Maybe then she'd have felt more of a bond.

It wasn't too late. That was something they could work on.

Except... did he want to work on it?

The sharpened knife edge of betrayal sliced painfully through his chest, accompanied by the blunt punch of distrust.

If she could go to this level of deception for something as massive and life changing as a child, what else might she do?

Lots of things in a relationship could be fixed with a little time and effort.

But trust? Once that was broken, it was hard to repair.

And his wasn't just broken, it had been sliced up into tiny little pieces, before being set on fire and the ashes that were left had washed away in the deluge of doubt and cynicism she'd unleashed.

Jenny had always made a point of taking Carys to her appointments before today. Ash had seen that as a positive thing. Now he wasn't sure if it was because she was trying to avoid anyone being on her back about her commitment to having a baby. Or if it had been to ensure he never discovered her duplicity, like he had done. Did she think enough time had passed that it wouldn't matter?

It all came down to trust and now he was second guessing everything.

The devil inside him made him hunt down her credit card statements, so he could verify her story.

The lack of trust reared its ugly head like a demon, but he had to be certain some other guy wasn't going to turn up on his doorstep one day, claiming paternal rights.

He paid the bill every month, but rarely took issue with anything she bought on his account. And since she didn't have an income of her own, he'd always allowed her the privacy of those statements, even though, technically, the cards were in his name because of her previous poor credit history. He'd thought that was important.

He found the entries for the fertility clinic. Finding out she'd told the truth about it didn't make him feel very much better.

Except... they started even before she'd brought up the subject of children and he'd denied her. The figure was always the same; a monthly payment plan by the look of it. Had she been hoping he'd change his mind, so her subterfuge wasn't so great? Or had she just been careful to ensure a lump sum payment didn't throw up a red flag?

Whatever her mindset had been, it turned out the joke was on him.

He'd paid for her to deceive him.

* * *

It was a couple of hours later when the knock on the door came. To begin with, he'd thought Jenny had forgotten her house keys.

The two police officers on his doorstep were a surprise; a man and a woman, their faces painted with practiced sympathy that had dread crystallising in his chest before they even spoke.

He didn't remember inviting them in. He didn't remember the conversation that led up to the words that changed his life forever.

"I'm sorry to tell you, your wife and daughter were both killed in a traffic collision, this afternoon. I'm sorry for your loss."

I'm sorry for your loss. The words were so trite they were almost meaningless. A tiny drop of commiseration measured against an oceanful of pain.

"What happened?" The words were hoarse and sounded distant even to his own ears.

His first thought was that Jenny had done something stupid. Something to expound the guilt he was already starting to feel. She was out there because of him, because he hadn't been able to stand the sight of her in light of her betrayal. If he hadn't sent her away, she'd still be here, safe.

Carys would still be here.

"I'm afraid her vehicle was hit head on by a drunk driver," the policewoman told him, fussing around and trying to comfort him. "He was killed too."

Was that supposed to make him feel better?

She sat him down and gave him a glass of water - like that would help! She asked if there was anyone she could call; anyone who could stay with him.

He shook his head. He didn't want anyone. He just wanted to be left alone with his grief and his regret.

He'd already felt ravaged before. Now he felt like a train wreck. He was still functioning, but the individual parts of his heart and soul were strewn around him and he didn't think he'd ever feel whole again.

And through it, all the vicious teeth of guilt ate at him.

This wasn't a storm; it was a tsunami. And it had crashed over him and left nothing but destruction in its path

Zack Kincaid & Daniella Moreno

Daniella 'Dani' Moreno put the final touches on the presentation she was preparing for her uncle.

Even she knew she'd outdone herself this time. This... this, was what was going to snag her the prodigious promotion she'd been working her butt off for the last six months.

You'd think with it being her uncle's company, she'd be a shoo-in, but her mother's brother had never been one for blind nepotism. Even his own son, her cousin, Luca, had worked his way up from pool boy in one or other of his father's resorts.

Of course, Luca had still scaled the ladder far quicker than Dani had, but she supposed that was to be expected, since Zio Lorenzo expected him to take over the company one day. Not that Luca wasn't good at his job, he was. Or that Lorenzo didn't send Luca on some equally random assignments. He did; like the 'mystery shopper' trips he insisted Luca take to check out their resorts as a customer.

But Luca was the apple of his father's eye, whereas Dani often felt like she was a piece of lint on his custom-tailored

137

suit. Sometimes she thought he wouldn't have given her a job at all, if her mother hadn't insisted she needed something constructive to do with her time.

For whatever reason, her Madre was under the mistaken assumption that Dani was going to burn through the inheritance her late father had left her, so she'd insisted the young Dani's time be filled to stop that from happening.

In fact, nothing could be further from the truth. She'd invested the money carefully and right now, thanks to Zack, it was probably worth three or four times the amount she'd been bequeathed. Enough that she could live off of the interest if she chose.

But damn it, she was excellent at her job. It wasn't just a filler or something she felt obliged to do because it was family.

She loved it. The hospitality industry was in her blood.

And not only did she deserve this promotion because of her own hard work and dedication, but there was no one even close to her level of competency. As far as Dani was concerned, it was pretty much in the bag.

But that didn't mean she could rest on her laurels. Doing an exceptional job was a matter of pride for her and she had a constant thirst to learn, to excel at every part of the business of running a resort, so she stood out as an all-rounder and could turn her hand to anything.

Thinking of Zack had her heart tripping, just as it always did. She was in love with him, of course. Not that she had any means of comparison, but the fact that the very idea of life without him seemed like an abyss of dread which scared her to death convinced her of the notion.

She smiled a secret smile at the thought of seeing him that night and hurried to finish her presentation so she could leave and get ready for her evening. It was true to say that Zack was the only thing that could drag her away from her work, too.

* * *

Zack walked into the club and looked around for Dani as he made his way towards the bar.

He always arranged to meet her here. Anything to avoid their hook-ups from seeming too much like a date.

It wasn't that he objected to their relationship heading into deeper territory. He would have preferred that if he were honest with himself. He was ready to settle down and start a family, but that was out of the question right now, from a moral point of view, if not a physical one. And he didn't want to lead her on by offering something he wasn't able to commit to fully.

Pushing the bitterness out of his mind, he resolved to enjoy their evening and the time they could spend together.

They were well matched when it came to kink. He'd met her here at this very club, twelve months ago, and in that time, things had evolved so that they were pretty much exclusive.

He'd resisted it at first. Didn't want to give her the wrong impression, but as time had marched on, he found himself less and less interested in entertaining other play partners, so on the rare occasion he did scene with someone else, there was never intercourse involved. He simply couldn't bear the thought of having sex with anyone but Dani. Like he was being unfaithful or something, even though they didn't have any kind of genuine relationship that extended beyond hooking up for a kink scene.

And wasn't that the ultimate irony.

He found her talking to another couple of subs and her face lit up when she saw him. It was like a balm to his battered soul.

He walked over and kissed her forehead when she jumped up to greet him. She felt like his safe place. With Dani, everything seemed simple. Oh, he knew it wasn't, but he liked the illusion. It allowed him those precious moments of peace.

She picked up two bottles of water and handed him one, then took his hand and started dragging him off towards the lounge area. Neither of them ever drank alcohol before they scened. He liked that she had the same attitude about that as he did. It was just another small way they fit.

"I wanted to talk to you about a business investment before we started," she told him, her face animated, and he could tell it was something she was enthusiastic about.

While he was an investment broker, his job normally consisted of matching the right people to the right kind of investment for them. Once that pairing was successful, he took a commission, and that was the end of his involvement.

Still, he knew his stuff and he could certainly advise Dani on whatever kind of enterprise had her so excited.

Since he doubled as a venture capitalist in his own right, it might even be something he was interested in. He was always on the search for new initiatives, and he had a knack for recognising those which showed promise and separating the wheat from the chaff. It was a talent that had made him a rich man.

"So, what's this investment you're interested in?" he asked as they sat down, and she snuggled into the crook of his arm.

It was a habit they'd developed, which was more than just Dom and sub, but they were both comfortable with it.

"My cousin, Luca, wants to buy a private island and set it up as a resort," she told him.

Zack frowned; he was familiar with her family business. Their resort chain was second to none. "You'll have to tell me a bit more, pet," he encouraged. "Because right now I'm just wondering why he's not just running it through the company."

"Well, the company belongs to Zio Lorenzo, and Luca wants this to be his baby," she replied.

Still not making sense. Yes, the company might belong to his father, but Luca Moreno was set to take over and, since he was the only heir, it wasn't like there was any doubt there.

"But mostly it's because he wants to set it up as a kink island, so it won't fit with the family resorts in Lorenzo's portfolio. Not even the adults, only ones."

Okay, now it made sense. It was an intriguing idea and one that tantalised him on a personal basis.

"Okay, this island... where is it, what's the size, the cost and the condition?" He slipped into business mode without even noticing.

Just like Dani slipped into her sales patter. "The island is approximately five miles by three miles in size, and it's in the Caribbean, approximately eighty miles east of Miami. Luca's negotiating the cost, but he's hoping to bring it in under ten million dollars. The island is uninhabited, completely empty, but that's what he wants. He's keen to set up the infrastructure from scratch so it works for the vision he's got for this place."

Zack knew Luca Moreno had both the knowledge and the contacts to pull the scheme off. There was no doubt in his mind about that.

However, building a resort from the ground up was going to take a huge influx of cash, way more than the initial seed money for the purchase of the island itself. It was going to need some very deep pockets, but Zack could see the definite advantages of setting up a kink resort that way.

"I think the big question is whether it would cover the investment with kink alone," he told Dani after some consideration. "Plus, you need to ask him if all those involved are going to be in the lifestyle. That's certainly the best way to do it. It circumvents any chance of misunderstanding between investors about the intricacies of the BDSM lifestyle. Certainly a project on this scale doesn't need someone pulling out because they don't understand the differences between consensual kink and abuse, and we all know that's a very real concern."

He scratched at the stubble he hadn't shaved, simply because Dani liked the feel of it against her skin, and continued. "If it was me, that's a condition I'd insist on to minimise the risk. It means finding the capital will take longer... but it would be worth it, though, for that kind of peace of mind."

Dani pursed her lips. "You're right, and he might even have already made that decision, but it's definitely something I need to find out. But what did you mean when you talked about whether the investment could be covered by kink alone?"

"I mean the outlay is going to be massive and the kink community - especially those who are going to be able to afford what I'm guessing is going to be a high-class resort, are going to be a fraction of the number of general holiday makers you and Luca are used to dealing with in your uncle's company. That makes it a catch twenty-two situation. The fewer visitors, the more you'll need to charge. The more you charge, the less people can afford it."

Dani plucked at her bottom lip, and a crease in the middle of her eyebrows marred her smooth complexion. "I see what you mean. But I'm not sure what the answer is," she revealed, a hint of worry creeping into her voice.

He hated to burst her bubble, but there were still options. "The island is big enough that you have the option to build two hotels that could be amply distanced from each other. One could be Luca's kink dream, the other could be a regular adult only venue which would bring in the cash."

"Actually, that's a great idea," she said, her excitement catching fire again.

"It also presents a number of options to create the kind of paradise even those in the lifestyle crave for more than just a kinky weekend, meaning they'd extend their breaks if there were additional facilities."

She flung her arms around him and pressed a quick kiss to his cheek. "You really should talk to Luca about this. You have so much insight," she whispered as she nibbled on his earlobe. "The two of you would make a great team."

The intoxicating smell of her perfume brought him back to the present and the fact that there was a private playroom upstairs with his reservation on it.

He didn't think she was necessarily trying to recruit him as an investor, but he had to admit, he was kind of tempted.

But right now, there were much more interesting things to explore. Surging to his feet, he pulled her up with him and headed for the stairs. It was time to give his little entrepreneur a reward for all her hard work.

* * *

"Strip off your clothing, Daniella," Zack demanded as soon as they'd closed the door of the suspension room behind them.

While his smooth flow from social into business mode had been seamless, his swap to Dom mode was like a switch being flipped and showed a completely different side of him.

One that made Dani's skin burst out into goosebumps and her abdomen clench in anticipation.

He took a skein of deep red rope from his toy bag. It was his favourite colour on her. He said it complemented her olive skin. It also meant he was feeling indulgent. He usually used black or plain hemp rope when he wasn't. And if he was in the mood for something particularly intricate, he used white for contrast.

Dani loved the feel of the rope. It was something that almost defied explanation. It was as if being bound set her free.

She worked long, hard hours and was always on the go. Shibari forced her to stop, to do nothing. To switch off for a few precious hours and just *feel*.

It worked as much for her overactive brain as it did for her hyperactive habits, and she had come to rely on it as a form of relaxation. It forced her out of her head, forced her to be still and quiet, and brought her a special kind of peace that she'd never found anywhere else.

She could feel the stresses of her working week starting to drain from her just at the thought of what was to come. She finished undressing and stood with her eyes closed, just soaking up the swirling, erotic atmosphere that simply being here with Zack created.

Sometimes he blindfolded her, but today was not one of those days.

Dani kept her eyes closed so she could absorb every subtle

nuance as he began draping her body in rope, decorating her with knots; so she could concentrate on the feel of the strands against her skin.

Sometimes rough, sometimes smooth; always tantalising.

He took his time, making sure every single twist and loop, every ligature and fastening, was perfect.

She forgot all her insecurities about her overly curvy body; her wide hips that weren't in balance with her average breasts, or the slight paunch of her stomach.

Zack made her feel beautiful.

Each coil of the rope around her body took her deeper within herself, to that special place where nothing but calm and tranquillity existed, until she felt like she was floating.

The squeeze around her breasts had her nipples pouting and throbbing like they were begging for his mouth. And the strategically placed knots which ran down her centre had already started their dastardly dilemma; rubbing against her clit and making her want to find just that little bit more friction, which would lead to the ultimate pleasure.

Except she was forbidden to come.

He didn't need to say it. It was an unspoken rule that in any scene they did; she didn't climax without permission.

If she did, he'd cut things short and instead of finishing the night with the deeply drugging satisfaction and irresistible intimacy of intercourse, he'd put her on her knees and fuck her face. Taking his own pleasure since she had constructed her own without him.

She'd made that mistake once and learned her lesson.

Plus, it was never as satisfying to steal a forbidden climax as it was to struggle against the eroticism until she received the ultimate prize of their passionate, carnal coupling. Nothing came close to touching her as deeply as that, and it was *so* worth the wait.

When he finished with the bindings, he took the next step;

attaching special pulley ropes with carabiner hooks fastened to them, so he could string her up and suspend her in whichever position it pleased him to fuck her in.

Today her arms were stretched together above her head and her ankles crossed and bound and connected to a rope that drew them up horizontally in front of her.

Zack pressed her knees apart, then ducked down and wedged his lean, runners' body in between so that he was enveloped within the circle of her legs.

He'd stripped naked himself and she could feel the heat of his skin against her own, the sensual rasp of flesh against flesh. Soft against hard.

She looked at his handsome face. His normally perfectly groomed hair flopped into his eyes, and he'd removed his glasses. It was the only time she ever saw him without them, and somehow that felt like another intimacy; something only she got to see.

His hands stroked reverently across her skin, over and in between his ropes, and she felt as cherished as if he were caressing some precious jewel. Mere words alone could never describe the sublime sensations he brought to her world. Perhaps that was why she'd fallen for him. He gave her so very much.

Was it selfish of her to want even more?

The thoughts scattered, washed away on the tide of desire when he leaned in and took one of her straining, pouting nipples into his mouth.

She choked on a gasp as pleasure flowed through her in molten rivers which swirled in her abdomen, then settled into her pussy, evidenced by the slick wetness that coated her thighs.

He took long, lazy suckles which ramped up her desire and had her writhing while the knot on her clit drove her dangerously close to the edge of a precipice she didn't want to topple over.

"Please..." she begged him, but his only answer was to nip at her sensitised flesh. The quick flash of pain was a double-edged sword. It cooled her lust on the one hand but had her bucking against the clit knot and stimulating that little bundle of nerves, unbearably, on the other.

His low chuckle told her he knew exactly the predicament she was in.

He took his sweet time and laved her other breast and Dani wiggled and panted and strained against her bonds; anything to prevent the spiral of arousal that would lead to her downfall.

Small whimpering sobs and nonsense words fell from her lips as her skin became clammy with the tell-tale bloom of lustful hunger.

"Please Sir, please," she implored. "I can't stop it any longer."

Still, he forced her closer to the edge, until desperation coloured her voice. Finally he took pity on her and drove into her dripping, clenching channel in a single, fluid thrust which almost forced her to topple over the precipice on which she balanced.

Dani screamed her frustration, letting out her pent-up feelings in the only other way she knew how.

Zack set up a frantic pace, using the rope suspension like a swing which allowed him to penetrate so deeply he bottomed out against her cervix with each and every powerful plunge. The momentum meant he forced the knotted rope to rub abrasively against her clit with every driving jolt, and the painful pressure had her flying even higher until she was sobbing in earnest.

She couldn't hold it any longer.

Her limbs were shaking with the effort of trying to hold

back the impossible tide which was about to crash over her, and her thighs quivered.

Finally, finally, he gave her the words she was desperate to hear. "Come, Daniella. Come now!"

And those words had her shattering, the pieces of her soul flying apart before they coalesced into a shimmering light and became whole again.

Zack let out a guttural groan and threw back his head, the strong column of his throat straining as the tendons in his neck tensed and he chased his own climax.

Later, when she was freed and cleaned up, he fed her squares of chocolate and sips of water while she snuggled into him and stroked his chest. She wished they were both still naked, but that was something that never seemed to be a part of his aftercare. He always ensured they were fully dressed before he settled.

She felt sated and lulled, and maybe that's why she spoke before she fully thought things through. Voicing something that had been on her mind for a while now.

"Zack," Dani began tentatively. "Do you think perhaps we could just... go out for a drink together or something, sometime? I mean nothing full on, just maybe see each other in a location, a situation, outside the club. It's just that we even discuss business here. It kind of feels awkward sometimes."

* * *

Zack sighed. He should have seen this coming. "I don't think that's a good idea, Dani," he said as gently as he could.

She looked hurt and confused, and for a moment, Zack was tempted to reconsider.

"But... why not?" she whispered. "I thought things were good between us. That we had something more than just shared kink going for us. Like maybe there could be more..."

"I agree, Dani. I feel the same way, but... things are... awkward."

She pulled out of his arms and frowned at him, her eyes narrowing. "I don't like the sound of that. What does that even mean?" she asked, and he could hear the suspicion that coloured her voice.

Damn it, this was not the way he wanted to have this conversation. He wasn't ready. He hadn't thought through the best way to tell her so that she'd understand; so he didn't mess everything up.

But perhaps it was best to have everything out in the open. There was no way he could enter into a relationship without telling her.

He sighed and took a leap of faith.

"I'm married," he told her, then winced. It sounded dreadful. Too blunt. He knew he should have waited to have this conversation until he was ready. Sometime when they weren't both blissed out by sex and kink and his brain was functioning on only half its blood flow because the rest had been expended by his cock.

"You're married?" she repeated in a shocked whisper, the blood draining from her face and leaving her pale, despite her tanned complexion.

"But... but you're getting divorced, right? You and your wife are finished, but the process isn't yet complete... right?" She said it with a hint of desperation, like she was clutching at straws.

Zack grimaced, and Dani's mouth fell open. "Not exactly," he told her truthfully. "It's complicated."

"How complicated can it be, Zack?" She scooted away from him now, jumping off the bed and putting a distance between them that was more than just physical. "You're either married or you're done with that relationship and terminating it. So just answer me honestly, are you getting divorced any time soon? That's all I need to know."

"I..." Zack closed his eyes and rubbed his hands over his face. This was not going to plan - not that he'd had any plan. But he'd hoped for better than this. He could already feel everything spiralling out of control.

He climbed off the bed himself. He needed to be close to her. To feel that bond they shared.

"Dani..." He exhaled a breath and took her in his arms. She allowed it, but he hated the rigidity he could feel in her frame. But she'd asked him for the truth. How could he give her anything less? "No, I'm not, but..." He didn't get any further.

"Then you're nothing but a nasty, lying cheat." She pushed him away from her so forcefully that he stumbled backwards.

"Look, I know it sounds bad, but it's not like that. Please, let me explain," he begged as she grabbed her belongings and headed for the door. He needed to tell her the whole story. What the hell had possessed him to start this conversation here, in a theme room of a kink club, where they were surrounded by people, and the privacy ended just as soon as she walked through that door?

Dani shook her head, her eyes a little wild and showing the tell-tale sheen of tears behind her fury. "Save it," she shouted as she fumbled with the latch. "I'm not interested. Just stay away from me, Zack. I don't do married men and I can't believe you've deceived me all this time. I can't believe you cheapened what we had by making me nothing more than a mistress to a cheater."

Zack closed his eyes in despair as the door slammed close behind her.

None of that had gone right. The words didn't come out the way he wanted, and everything had been twisted.

This was why he'd always kept his distance. Was she right, though? Was he a cheat?

He didn't think he was, but then maybe he was biased. But how the hell could he be faithful to a girl he'd been coerced into marrying when he was just fifteen years old. Not even officially an adult. And his 'bride', and he used the term with caution, had been only fourteen. He'd met her for the first time that same day, for maybe fifteen minutes, and he hadn't seen her since.

All because his father and her mother had signed some kind of contract and given their consent for the underage marriage of their children.

And yes, it was legal!

Right here in the United States, it was legal. He'd had a lawyer check into it years ago, when the full significance of the deed had finally dawned on him.

To this day, the USA had marriage laws which allowed children as young as twelve to be married with their parents' permission. Younger, though that was rare.

Who knew!

And the contract was legally binding as well. He'd checked that too, hoping it could be voided on the grounds that he hadn't agreed. But since he was a minor at the time, it seemed his father had all the rights. He had to remain married to Emylyah Kincaid nee Baskov for twenty years before he could seek an annulment.

And he still had another few years to wait.

Zack wondered if he should go after Dani and try to make her listen. But truth be known, he was angry with her, too, for storming out without giving him the chance to explain. For not having enough faith in him to realise the truth was far more involved than the simple yes or no answer she had demanded.

If she couldn't give him at least that much, then what was the point in prostrating himself for someone who didn't want to listen?

Perhaps, despite her pretty words, she didn't care enough to want to find out. He saw it all the time in his line of business; how people said they wanted something but changed their minds when it wasn't as straight forward or as easy as they thought it would be.

But even if she did, what did he have to offer? It might be a technicality, but he *was* still a married man.

She was right in that much, at least.

Maybe it was better this way.

Better to just let things go and see if here were any pieces worth picking up when he was finally in a position to pursue her.

And if there weren't, well, he guessed it would never have worked out in the first place, and maybe they'd just saved themselves a whole lot more heartache.

But there was at least one way he could keep tabs on her until he finally became a free man.

Picking up the phone, Zack looked up the number for Dani's cousin, Luca Moreno, and dialled it.

"Moreno," the disembodied voice on the other end of the phone introduced.

"Hello, Mr Moreno, I'm Zack Kincaid. I'm an investment broker and your cousin, Daniella, was telling me about your new kink resort project. She says you're looking for investors with initial seed money of one million dollars. I'd like to buy into it as a silent partner."

* * *

Dani threw herself into her work. If there was one area where she was confident, then it was here. And what better way to prep for that promotion than to throw in a few extra hours?

Besides, if she tired herself out, she didn't have to think about what a lying, cheating bastard Zack Kincaid was. She didn't have time to concentrate on how much her heart hurt and why she couldn't understand how she'd read him so wrong. Because he'd never come across as someone who had a wife at home or like he was sneaking around behind someone's back.

She erased all those questions from her mind. It didn't matter. Facts were facts, and those had been established.

No point in crying over spilt milk. The damage was already done. She gave herself the pep talk at the same time as she brushed away yet another tear; one more to add to the sea she'd already cried along with all those other platitudes she'd quoted to herself.

Plenty more fish in the sea.

Narrow escape.

Every cloud has a silver lining.

Blessings in disguise.

Better to have loved and lost that never to have loved at all. She wasn't sure if she believed that one yet.

It didn't matter though, she told herself determinedly. It just meant she had more time to dedicate to her job. She was going to need it once she got this promotion, because there was going to be a huge amount to do to launch the new marketing plan she was putting to the board this afternoon. It was the most ambitious proposal she'd ever delivered, but she was confident that it was also ingenious and would set their top line at an all-time high. But it was complicated, so she'd be needing all that extra time to put it into action. If she told herself that enough, she might start believing it.

So, she dried her eyes, touched up her make-up and dived into her presentation with the plan to knock their socks off.

And she did.

Even Zio Lorenzo was impressed, and he was always a hard sell.

"Ah! Daniella. This is truly inspired," he congratulated, and Dani could feel his faith in her filling up all the empty places Zack's departure had left.

She was going to be fine.

There was a babble around the room as the board members commented and complimented her, and all of it buoyed her and filled Dani with a new hope for the future.

Luca got up from his seat, right in front of everyone, and gave her a hug; told what a brilliant job she had done.

Everything was going to be all right.

Lorenzo started talking again, and everyone settled down. "While we're all here, this seems like the most opportune time to announce the promotions I promised."

Dani's heart soared. This was it. Everything she'd ever worked for. She'd delivered a presentation that had impressed everyone, and now she was going to get her reward.

She didn't need Zack Kincaid. She had all she needed right here.

Everything was going to be perfect.

Lorenzo announced a couple of the minor roles, and there was muted applause with each one. Then it was time for hers. She held her breath, almost unable to contain her excitement. She felt like she might burst, but that would have to come later. Right now, she needed to behave like the consummate professional.

"And finally, I'd like to announce the promotion for the position of Promotions Director."

There was a hushed silence around the room. It was the first time a directorship had become available in all the years Dani had been working here, and that was over a decade. Well, not unless you counted Luca's, but that had been a made-up post, because he was the owner's son and future heir. There wasn't likely to be another coming up anytime soon.

"As I'm sure you're all aware, this is a very important and prominent position, so I've given it a great deal of thought." Lorenzo droned on, and Dani wished he'd just get on with it. She hated all this suspense.

"I'm sure you'll all agree that the best person for the job is..."

He paused, smiling from ear to ear, milking the build-up before he announced, with a flourish.

"Justin James."

There was muted, almost awkward applause as the man in question popped up and pumped her uncle's hand.

Dani felt like there was a loud roaring sound in her ears and everything seemed to be happening in slow motion.

For a long, long moment she stood there, right next to what they'd said was her amazing presentation, completely stunned.

Her mouth hung open, her eyes widened in sheer disbelief and shock coursed through her body on a surge wave of adrenaline until her brain finally caught up with the events that unfolded before her, and the shock was replaced with the kind of fatal anger that wiped out every other emotion.

In her peripheral vision, her subconscious catalogued the uncomfortable shuffling of several other board members as they looked from her to an oblivious Lorenzo, to Justin.

Even Luca's handsome face was a rictus of surprise, then

annoyance, proving that he'd been left out of this equation, too.

If looks could kill... now there was another metaphor that was going to be used today.

Dani turned her furious gaze on Lorenzo, and even he had the awareness to look taken aback by the lethal venom that must be pouring off of her.

"Is this your idea of a joke?" she asked in a voice that dripped ice. And she was damn proud of how composed and calm she sounded, when underneath that veneer of surface calm she was a seething mass of boiling anger.

"I've worked all hours to bring you the best marketing plan ever, and you give my promotion to someone who's worked here half the years I have and has a fraction of my experience?"

"Now, now dear," Lorenzo said in that obsequious tone that proved he was just humouring her. "What's the good in promoting you into a man's job, when you'll just end up leaving to pop out babies as soon as you find yourself a husband?"

"Papa..." Luca's shocked voice issued a warning to his father, but Dani didn't hear anything that was said over the eruption of shocked, murmured whispers that buzzed around the room.

She clenched her jaw as a red haze swam before her eyes. She fisted her hands and held them rigidly at her sides because the urge to lash out, physically, and transfer some of the hurt that was currently overwhelming her was a very real threat.

The straw that broke the camels' back. Now there was a very pertinent idiom; because that was her.

No more.

No more would she slog her guts out just to have the rug pulled out from under her feet just when she thought she'd reached her goal.

Things crystallised for her then. She'd never be anything, in her uncles' eyes, except a little woman who would one day run off and have babies, which was exactly what her place should be.

No matter how hard she worked, or how hard she tried, he was too blinkered to see her value.

Well, so be it. If he thought he could manage without her so easily, then he could start right now.

Hell hath no fury like a woman scorned. That was something her uncle would do well to mind.

"I quit," she said through gritted teeth, and suddenly the room was quiet enough to hear a pin drop.

"Now don't be so ridiculous and melodramatic, Daniella," her uncle reprimanded.

He just didn't get it.

He shook his head and looked at her as if she were a difficult child who needed to be cajoled. "I still need you to assist Justin in getting your marketing plan up and running."

She stared at him through eyes narrowed to slits. "Well, I'm sure since you think Justin is more competent and deserving of a directorship than I am, that he'll be perfectly capable of handling it himself." Dani sneered, derision dripping from her voice like poison.

He wouldn't, but she'd be damned if she spent one more fraction of a second on anyone who didn't appreciate her worth. And if her uncle came to regret it, then perhaps he'd learn a valuable lesson. One far too long in coming.

Picking up her purse, she turned on her heel. She didn't bother stopping at her office. There was nothing she needed to take with her.

Instead, she walked right on out of the building for what she swore to herself would be the last time.

It was time to find something else to do with her life.

There was nothing left for her here anymore.

Not in this company; not in this city.

Luckily, she knew a brand-new island resort that might just have an opening for someone with her skill set.

Saul Stephens

S aul watched the first handprint bloom on the bare buttocks of the girl he had tied to the massive bed in his luxury hotel suite and felt pleasure unfurl in his chest.

Everything about her did it for him.

Her pale skin which marked so beautifully.

The lush roundness of her ass and her curves that went on for days.

The way her heavy tits swung with every movement, from how he had her positioned on her knees.

Each of her arms was outstretched and bound to the wrought iron frame, as far apart as was still comfortable... but not too comfortable, he thought, with a wicked grin.

It gave him an impeccable view.

Her knees were spread. Not too wide to be uncomfortable, but enough that if he spanked her just right, it would catch her pouting pussy lips and add a little extra zing.

As eager as she'd been, he wasn't convinced she was a true submissive, so he was treading carefully and not taking things past light bondage and a bit of sexy spanking. The kind of things that might appear in any bedroom games. He'd get his real fix the next time he made it to a BDSM club, but this was enough to tide him over. He had a voracious sexual appetite, and he didn't apologise for it.

He was in London right now. In twelve hours' time, he'd be in Key West, Florida. He had no plans to sleep. He could do that in the comfort of his private Gulfstream jet during the ten-hour flight.

He knew his reputation as a billionaire playboy preceded him, and most women saw one as a handy entree to the other, hitting him up for sex in the hope of getting closer to his wallet.

He wasn't bitter about it. It was what it was.

Pretty much anyone who had enough interest to follow his well-publicised exploits also knew that it didn't work.

Oh, he enjoyed what the ladies had to offer all right, but he was strictly one and done.

But he was philosophical too, and he also had a reputation for being generous.

So, he'd wine and dine them and treat them to a bit of a shopping spree or let them keep his casino winnings... before he fucked their brains out and sent them on their way.

The odd one might have decided there should have been more and sold their story to the paparazzi - although he was always careful to tell them exactly how it was going to be. But really, that only added to the image he liked to keep, so it didn't bother him at all.

In reality, he prided himself on never leading any of them on. If they thought they could change him... well, that was on them. He never promised more than he was prepared to give. Ever.

And what he promised was a night of scintillating sex and some extravagant perks.

He'd already wined and dined... Shelly? Sheri? Sharon? He

couldn't remember her name, but that wasn't unusual either. He generally went with a generic 'babe' for every woman he met. It circumvented the risk of any hurt feelings. Saul might be a bit of a player, but he didn't want that.

Women were to be cherished... he just liked to cherish rather a lot of them.

Usually after he'd thrashed them soundly and turned them into a begging, blubbering wreck.

He and his current playmate had hit the hotel casino after food, and he'd popped a stack of chips into her purse and asked her to look after them for him. She probably didn't know it, but there was probably five or six thousand pounds worth. He wouldn't be asking for it back.

Saul treated her other buttock to the same treatment as the first; enjoyed the give of her ample curves and the blossoming pink impression his hand made on her other cheek. She squealed, and he was quick to soothe. Rubbing the abused flesh, he crooned to her in his bedroom voice.

"There's a good girl. Just a few more for me, baby. Then I'm going to make you feel *sooo* good."

She took a couple more, but he felt like she was just tolerating them for him, so he switched it up and curled himself over her back until he could palm the weight of her breast. Their luscious bounty overspilled his hands, but he massaged them as he pressed his pelvis against the heat he'd instilled in her ass. God, he loved that sensation. The spanks he'd given her were light enough that it was fading fast, but he enjoyed it while it lasted, the hard length of his cock notching into the crease of her ass. He doubted very much she'd be up for anal, which was a bit sad. But he didn't have the time to prepare a neophyte.

He drew his thumbs across her nipples until they stood out like hard, proud berries. She had a glorious pair of tits. It was almost a pity she wasn't in a position where he could suckle on them. He would have liked to have buried his head in her generous globes.

Saul made do with pulling and pinching at them until she was bucking and panting beneath him. One hand wandered south, and he fluttered his fingers over the short, trimmed hair of her mons, teasing deliberately.

"Oh god, please..." she begged in between her panting breaths. She wasn't quite as experienced as his normal pickups. He'd had the impression she was surprised when he flirted with her at the hotel bar where she'd been sitting alone, staring into her drink, looking like she'd been stood up.

He didn't know her story; didn't want to. But she might be surprised to know that she was everything he adored in a woman. She wasn't skinny. She enjoyed her food. She was one heck of a conversationalist once she opened up and obviously had a good brain on her. She wasn't groomed to within an inch of her life, so that if you looked behind the makeup, you might not even recognise the same person.

Everything about her was real.

It would probably be a shock to the world and his dog to know that was his preference.

He took pity on her and rubbed his fingers around her hardened clit. The little noises that fell from her lips were addictive, along with the string of nonsense words and the little gasping breaths she huffed out.

If he were to hazard a guess, he'd bet that few men in her life had ever paid this much attention to her pleasure.

He could feel her thighs quivering and knew she was on the brink of orgasm, but she wasn't getting it that easily. Where would be the fun in that?

Instead, he lifted his fingers away from her clitoris and chuckled at her disappointed whimpers. "Oh... no, please. Come back!"

"Greedy girl. Don't you know that good things come to

those who wait?" he murmured into her ear before grazing the lobe with his teeth.

She shuddered, and he circled her labia with two fingers until she was whimpering for an entirely different reason.

When she started to mewl and tried to hump against his hand, he withdrew completely and gave her a couple more well-placed spanks that had her crying out again.

Then he plunged his fingers into her wet, honeyed depths, curling them so they hit her sweet spot. If she hadn't been tied down, he thought she might have bucked off the bed at that point. Yeah, the men in her life had been severely lacking, if her surprise was anything to go by. He hoped after tonight she got a bit more demanding about her pleasure. Now she knew the g-spot wasn't a myth.

Grabbing a condom from the side table where he'd left a pile of them, he tore open the packet with his teeth and sheathed himself with an ease born from years of practice.

"Are you ready for me, baby?" he asked, plucking at her nipples again. She writhed and undulated, pulling against her bindings.

"Yes! Oh, yes. Please," she choked out in near desperation, wiggling her ass against him.

"I'm going to fuck you hard, baby. Is that what you want? Do you want my cock pounding into your tight little cunt like a jackhammer?"

"Yes!" she shrieked, arching her back and pushing out her rear in a desperate offering. "Now! Please!"

If a submissive in the club had made such demands, he'd have made her wait. Maybe edged her for a while. But this little beauty was more reminiscent of a suburban housewife or a librarian. And he was going to shake her world.

He took his sheathed cock in his hand and drew it up and down her creamy slit. But that was all the warning she got. Notching his cock head, he drove into her in one smooth but forceful thrust, then set up a punishing pace as he hammered into her.

Her squeals and moans became a constant, high-pitched scream and Saul was thankful he had the penthouse suite which took up the entire top floor, so they didn't disturb anyone, or have the staff banging on the door thinking he was killing her.

The bed rocked against the wall and Saul gripped her hips as he fucked into her with strong, deep strokes, which bottomed out each time.

He felt her start to flutter and tighten around his shaft and reached around to pinch her clit.

That was all it took.

Throwing back her head, she screamed her pleasure loud and long. Saul grabbed a handful of her hair and tilted her head to one side before sinking his teeth into that spot where her neck met her shoulder just as she was ebbing, and that seemed to set her off again.

He smoothed his hand down the sweaty length of her spine and felt his own climax take hold, but held it back for several long moments, allowing it to build, before letting out a roar of completion.

Her breathing was ragged and her chest heaving when he pulled out.

Saul made quick work of disposing of the condom and then hurried to undo her bindings.

She collapsed into a heap on the bed and Saul was pretty sure she wasn't going to move for a good long time. And that meant he'd done his job well.

Snatching a couple of bottles of water from the fridge, he sat one on the bedside table next to her and took a couple of gulps of his own before he crawled in beside her.

She curled up like a satisfied kitten in his arms and Saul smiled, enjoying the feel of her.

He woke her several more times in the night and took his pleasure over again, showering her with more of her own. And he finally got to enjoy the bounty of her breasts for a good long time.

He snoozed a little in between, but by the time dawn broke he was awake, and she was dead to the world in the sleep of the exhausted.

Saul got up and showered. Then he phoned room service and instructed them to let her stay as long as she liked, and ordered her a breakfast of toast, scrambled eggs, bacon, and orange juice to be delivered at eleven am.

He grabbed his luggage and checked around the room to see if he'd forgotten anything. And still she slept, snoring ever so quietly.

Plucking a single white rose from the huge arrangement in the lounge, he dried the stem and made sure there were no thorns before he placed it gently on the pillow he'd just vacated.

He watched her sleeping for a few moments, then leaned in, kissed her forehead, and silently wished her a good life.

Then he walked out of the suite without another thought or as much as a backwards glance.

* * *

L ess than twenty-four hours later, Saul eyed the two skinny blondes who lay sunning themselves on the deck of his luxury yacht, as he guided the vessel away from Key West.

Macy and Donna... Marci and Dana?

Whatever. They were like twin Barbie dolls, he thought to himself. Fake boobs that made them look top heavy. Equally fake hair which reached down their backs in highlighted beachy waves; he'd have to be careful not to pull that too hard when he fucked one of them. And fake tan that gave them a slight orange tinge. He idly wondered if the real Caribbean sun would make that look better or worse.

They couldn't be more different from the woman he'd left sleeping that morning in London.

He'd almost slipped up and called one of them Barbie at one point. He wasn't convinced they'd see it as an insult, though, even if they understood the implication, so perhaps it didn't matter. It was close to 'baby'.

Hell, they were completely honest about who and what they were. High class call girls who made their money by being up for anything.

For the right price.

And he really did mean anything.

That's why he'd paid the big bucks for them to enjoy a luxury weekend aboard this floating playground of his. That honesty was more than could be said about a lot of the people he met, and he respected that about them.

The same couldn't be said for his other guest.

Manuel Ortega was a pimple on the backside of humanity. A drug lord and gun runner who thought he was above the law. The odious little man had a classic Napoleon complex, the small man syndrome, where lack of stature made him prone to violence and aggression to make up for his physical shortcomings.

He had warned Macy about Ortega before he'd hired her. She said she could handle him, but Saul was still cautious. She might be a body for hire, but he didn't want her to get hurt and Manuel had a reputation for liking it rough.

Of course, so did Saul, but consensual kink was a whole other ball game. He resolved to give her a bonus if things got out of hand, but he hoped it wouldn't come to that. He had a few tricks up his sleeve if the sleaze ball started to play up. He didn't want to use them. It would jeopardise this whole endeavour, but he'd do that before he allowed anyone to get hurt on his watch.

But he still had to balance that with the number of nameless, faceless people who would suffer if things didn't go to plan.

He gave an inward sigh and poured more champagne into Ortega's glass. Hopefully, the more incapacitated he was, the better. He was certainly banking on that to get the man's loose lips flapping.

Saul wasn't stupid. He knew damn well Manuel Ortega was hoping to get his clammy little hands on a whole lot of Saul's money for his slimy, underground investments.

The overlord saw Saul as a someone with more money than sense. An easy target to separate from a couple of million bucks with some half assed play and big promises that he probably couldn't keep. But that wouldn't bother him, because he didn't see Saul as any kind of threat who might come looking for his seed money.

A fool and his money were soon parted. That's how Manuel viewed Saul. Of course, if he had any real sense, he might stop to wonder why Saul was richer now than he'd ever been, because if you applied the tired cliche then he'd be broke by now.

Ortega had been courting Saul for months and Saul had repeatedly put him off with the excuse that he was jetting to some different part of the world. Which he had been, but he could have made the time in his life of partying if it had been important enough.

In fact, it had been more important to string Manuel along, then offer this particular weekend aboard Saul's yacht when they knew Ortega's cartel had a massive weapons deal purported to be going down.

It was a long shot. There was a huge chance their intel was wrong, or that he'd refuse the invitation, or maybe postpone the drop. They still didn't know if that had happened, but Saul guessed it would become obvious as things progressed.

In the meantime, there was champagne, women, a chef's buffet, and the entire place was wired for sound. Not that he was drinking himself, but he was putting on a good show with a second bottle of non-alcoholic Champagne he'd switched the labels on.

"So," Manuel asked, in his heavily accented voice. "When are you going to invest with me?" He rolled his R's and shortened his vowels, but underneath it all, Saul could hear that he was also starting to slur his words.

Diminished faculties made for flapping tongues as far as Saul was concerned.

"Ah, Manuel. But you haven't told me what I'm inveshtin' in yet, and what my returnsh gonna be," Saul slurred his own words to match and lifted his champagne flute to salute the other man before making a big show of downing it in one and refilling his glass, sloshing it deliberately as he did so.

Manuel narrowed his beady little eyes and Saul noticed a devious light come into them. Perhaps he wasn't the only one playing at being drunk. Well, more drunk than he really was, anyway. Saul knew exactly how many times he'd refilled Ortega's glass.

"Don't you worry about the small details, my friend. Manuel will take care of you personally and make sure the profit is always good."

Saul resisted the urge to roll his eyes. The man must think he was born yesterday. But then, that was all part of the front.

"How much you want?" Saul asked, without commenting on the terms.

Manuel grinned big, his teeth flashing white against his tanned skin. "How 'bout two mill, to start?" he said, his eyes trained on Saul's reactions. "Gotta be cash though."

Saul scrunched up his face and closed one eye, as if he was trying to focus. "Don' carry that much cash 'round wi' me dude," he replied before lumbering to his feet and weaving his way below deck. He went to the safe in the master cabin and drew out a stack of notes, before wandering back on deck.

He pulled a couple of hundreds out of one of the bundles and stuffed them lewdly down Macy and Donna's bikini tops, giving them a lascivious grin before he turned and tossed the rest to Manuel. "Here ya go. Have to take half a mill up front 'til I can get to a bank,"

Ortega's eyes lit up, and he groped after the money with his fat, meaty fingers. What he didn't know was that, in the unlikely event that he managed to get the money away somewhere before Saul's colleagues picked him up in the mainland sting operation, each note had been tagged and the serial numbers noted.

The mid-day sun was scorching down on them, and Saul was beginning to sweat. "S'too hot up here," he grumbled. "Gonna go take a siesta."

He turned to the two Barbies. "You two should do the same," he told them, wiggling his eyebrows. "When I wake up I'm gonna be hungry, an' not jus' for food."

He pointed towards the guest rooms they'd changed their clothing in, and they did as he suggested, like good little dolls.

He saluted Manuel before he went below deck, but the man was too busy checking the cash to take much notice.

Perfect.

As he slipped into his room, Saul flipped the switch on the recording system. He knew better than to keep it on when there was a chance he might incriminate himself. There was always some new kid on the block who didn't know the whole story and would try to prove that Saul's billions were the product of ill-gotten gains, even though every penny was legit.

He picked up a tiny earpiece and switched it on, tapping against it three times. That was his code to the team that the plan was a go.

Then he undid his white, short-sleeved shirt and the tie on his elasticated board shorts before settling down on his bed to wait.

He listened while Manuel Ortega made one hushed phone call after another, thinking he was completely alone and out of earshot. Which, in any other circumstance, he would have been.

Then, when he'd said enough to incriminate himself, Saul put the second part of the plan into place.

With the aid of a tiny, concealed jammer, he blocked the satellite signals to the boat, removed his earpiece, which he stowed carefully back in the safe, then lay back on the bed to pretend he was asleep.

He heard the shouting up on deck first. They were purposefully out in the middle of the ocean with no land in sight, although he doubted Ortega had any idea how close they actually were to land.

Next came the hammering on the door and Saul prepared himself to play his part once more.

"Stephens?" Manuel bellowed, as he loomed in the doorway.

"Here, let me," Donna said in a conciliatory voice as she ducked under Ortega's arm and into the room.

She shook him gently. "Saul? Saul, wake up!" she whisper shouted.

Saul grunted and tried to turn over, but she was persistent.

"'S'up?" he finally croaked out, groggily.

"Mr Ortega has a problem with his phone," she murmured, and he could hear by the edge of concern in her voice that Manuel was starting to throw his weight around.

Still...

"'S'not my problem his phone's crap," he slurred, shrugging her off.

She was pulled bodily away from him, and Saul gritted his teeth at Manuel's heavy handedness, burying his face in the pillow so his expression wasn't obvious.

"Stephens..." the other man blasted, clearly trying to intimidate. He was about to find out that wasn't going to happen.

Saul snapped his head around and glared at Manuel. "Fuck off, Ortega. I'm sleepin'," he spat. All hints of gullible 'Mr Nice Guy' gone.

The Cuban obviously realised that he might be jeopardising his other one point five million, because he immediately backed off.

"Saul, Saul... my sincere apologies," he said with sickening obsequiousness, his palms raised in supplication. "You misunderstand. This is an emergency. I just got word that my niece was rushed to hospital, and then I lost my phone signal."

Huh! So that's how he was playing it.

Saul made a show of wiping his hands over his face and rubbing his eyes. Then he sat up and swung his legs over the side of the bed. "Why didn't you just say so, man," he grumbled grumpily. "We're probably too far from land to pick up a signal. Let me grab a shower and something to eat and I'll manoeuvre us closer to shore.

Ortega looked like he might argue, but Saul thew him his best 'pissed off' face and stumbled into the shower room, allowing Ortega to think that he wasn't in any fit state to drive the boat right now.

As if he'd ever plot a course out to sea when he was under the influence. But this man didn't know that. To him, Saul was nothing but an international, billionaire playboy who partied hard.

Saul took his time. Now that they had the recordings of Ortega's phone conversations, he needed to give the ground crew as much time as possible to execute the sting without Manuel getting wind of it and disappearing in a moonlight flit. That was the other reason they were out on the yacht. Difficult to escape when you're surrounded by sea.

Someone had obviously taken him at his word, because when he finally surfaced there was a small plate of food and a steaming cup of coffee waiting for him, though he doubted Manuel had fixed it.

Saul ate while the other man paced impatiently. When he judged the Cuban was about out of patience, he forestalled his temper by going up onto the bridge and bringing the boat about in a wide arc until they were headed in the opposite direction.

That seemed to appease Ortega for a while, though he still checked for a signal every few minutes.

"Go fix Manuel something to eat," he called to Macy. Hopefully, feeding him would distract the man for a little while.

When it became clear that Manuel's temper was almost at snapping point, Saul sent the girls below deck, out of the firing line and manoeuvred the yacht towards port. As he expected, the sight of land on the horizon calmed things down immediately, even if he was still cursing that he couldn't get hold of anyone.

"Chill Manuel," Saul said soothingly. "You know they don't allow phones in hospitals. It doesn't necessarily mean there's anything wrong."

"What the hell are you talking about?" Ortega snapped.

"Your niece," he replied, the picture of innocence. "It's not necessarily bad news, just because you can't get hold of anyone. They make you switch your phone off in the hospital, don't they?"

Manuel scowled at him like he was mad, then his face cleared. "Oh, right, yes," he agreed, slipping his phone back into his pocket and standing by the rail so he could watch their passage into the harbour.

When they docked, he could barely leave the boat quickly enough. "I'm sorry, Saul, I'll be in touch," he said hurriedly as he hurried down the gangplank.

"No problem," Saul replied, raising his hand in a wave as Ortega hurried away without a backward glance.

* * *

S aul wasn't hanging around to remain in the crossfire. As soon as everything was clear, he drew back the gang-plank and turned the boat back out to sea. His involvement here was finished. A major cartel player had been lured onto US soil, where he could be arrested after incriminating himself, and it was time for Saul to make himself scarce.

"Well, it's a pity old Manuel couldn't stay," he told Macy and Donna an hour later, when he lowered the anchor in the shelter of a quiet cove and invited them to sit down to a proper dinner with him.

From the looks they were giving him, they obviously weren't too upset by the turn of events.

Sitting down, one on each side of him, they both had their hands all over him by the time the buffet was finished.

He wondered how hard they'd let him spank them. Might as well ask. After all, there was no point in wasting a perfectly good meal when it had already been paid for, Saul thought with a wicked grin. And he wasn't talking about the type of meal that involved food.

That particular hunger had been sated. Now it was time to take care of the other one. After all, not *all* of his playboy reputation was a lie. And it had been a while since he'd enjoyed two women at once.

Two hours later his iWatch beeped with a message and he gave a tired yawn as he tried to extricate himself from the two women for long enough to check it. Macy and Donna had been superb, much as he expected, and now they were both sleeping on either side of him.

He gave a satisfied smile when he read the text confirming the raid had been a success and Ortega had been intercepted and arrested before he left Key West on his way back to Cuba.

Saul stretched his tired muscles and moved around to try and get comfortable. God, he was tired.

For the first time in his life, he just wanted a relaxing bath and to go to bed - alone - and sleep.

As he closed his eyes and gave in to the exhaustion, the thought flitted through his mind that maybe he was getting too old for this.

Perhaps it was time to start searching for a different adventure.

Masters of
Paradise

Temptation

Surprise Pregnancy

Ash and Lucy are two lost souls both running from their past. They've sworn of relationships for good reason, but the temptation of a holiday fling is too great to withstand.

Resurrection

Christmas in Paradise

Trying, unsuccessfully, for a baby is tearing Sam and Sophie's relationship apart. So Sophie's sister, Lucy, and her husband Ash, treat the couple to a holiday in paradise as a chance to reconnect. Maybe it will also result in a Christmas miracle.

Valentine in Paradise

BBW Reverse Harem

Bethany is a big, beautiful woman with a kinky streak who wants to cross a very specific item off her bucket list.

Her very own reverse harem experience.

But it's not something she can do at home, so she sets off for the island of Elysium to make her dreams come true in paradise.

Scandal (March 2022)

Age Gap.

Dallas Johnson has already weathered one scandal. He doesn't need another. But when the lawyer who saved his hide comes to work for the Eden Resort sparks fly.

The trouble is, Mia is young enough to be his daughter.

Angel in Hades (May 2022)

On a blustery night in Detroit, Duke Marcus Mountbatten met a woman who looked like an angel.

He never expected to see her again. Turns out, he was wrong.

Dirty Dancing (July 2022)

Enemies to lovers.

Shelley is a pole dancer at the kink club, Iniquity.

Cree Smith is the head chef.

It's not her fault she keeps awkward hours, so why does the handsome chef always get bent out of shape when she wants to eat after her performances?

Bound in Paradise (September 2022)

Second chance romance.

Unwittingly married at fifteen in some crazy scheme cooked up by his father, Zack Kincaid has waited twenty years to be free of the child wife he met just once and never saw again.

Once he's gotten an annulment, he plans to make Dani Moreno listen to his story, even if he has to tie her up to do so.

But will the appearance of his child bride throw a spanner in the works.

International Playboy (November 2022)

Romantic suspense.

Saul Stephens has a reputation to maintain, but a bullet has other ideas for him and he takes refuge on the island of Elysium where a sassy nurse does more than save his life.

* * *

Each book in the series is a standalone with its own Happy Ever After. There are no cliffhangers, but you will meet lots of other characters who will have their own stories.

This is the list for the next twelve month. There are more titles to be added.

Reading order and dates are approximate and may be subject to change.

About the Author

Poppy Flynn was born in Buckinghamshire, UK and moved to Wales at eight years old with parents who wanted to live the 'self-sufficiency' lifestyle.

Poppy's love of reading and writing stemmed from her parents' encouragement and the fact that they didn't have a television in the house.

"When you're surrounded by fields, cows and sheep, no neighbours, no TV and the closest tiny village is four miles away, there's a certain limit to your options, but with books your adventures and your horizons are endless."

Poppy x

Join in the fun at her FB Reader Group
Sexy Spanking Reads.

Or search **Poppy Flynn** on Social Media

Also by
Poppy Flynn

Club Risqué Series: Each a standalone with its own Happily Ever
After.

Club Risqué Series

1. **Fool's Desire**
2. **Fear's Whisper**
3. **Ties that Bind**
4. **Dark Consequences**
5. **Friends with Benefits**
6. **Captive Heart**
7. **Tormented Dreams**

On His World Book 1 in a standalone spanking sci-fi trilogy

Smokin' Cowboys: Book 1 in the *Loved by Three* multi-author
reverse harem series.

Stranded with the Storm Chasers: Book 9 in the *Loved by Three*
multi-author reverse harem series.

Serendipity Series: A humorous witch academy series with adult
themes. Each book is a complete story following the misadventures
of Seren Starlight, but there is an arc of romance and mystery which
develops throughout the set.

1. *Serendipity:* **Samhain & Sorcery**
2. *Serendipity*: **Yule & Enchantment**
3. *Serendipity*: **Imbolc & Incantations**

Printed in Great Britain
by Amazon